I0534062

THE MASTER
OF SILENCE

A Romance

Irving Bacheller

1st WORLD
LIBRARY
Literary Society

The Master of Silence

Irving Bacheller

© 1st World Library – Literary Society, 2004
PO Box 2211
Fairfield, IA 52556
www.1stworldlibrary.org
First Edition

LCCN: 2005901332

Softcover ISBN: 1-4218-1147-2
Hardcover ISBN: 1-4218-1047-6
eBook ISBN: 1-4218-1247-9

Purchase *"The Master of Silence"*
as a traditional bound book at:
www.1stWorldLibrary.org/purchase.asp?ISBN=1-4218-1147-2

1st World Library Literary Society is a nonprofit
organization dedicated to promoting literacy by:

- Creating a free internet library accessible from any
  computer worldwide.
- Hosting writing competitions and offering book
  publishing scholarships.

Readers interested in supporting literacy
through sponsorship, donations or
membership please contact:
literacy@1stworldlibrary.org
Check us out at: www.1stworldlibrary.ORG
and start downloading free ebooks today.

The Master of Silence
contributed by Tim, Ed & Rodney
in support of
1st World Library Literary Society

CHAPTER I

Near the end of my fourteenth year I was apprenticed to Valentine, King & Co., cotton importers, Liverpool, as a "pair of legs." My father had died suddenly, leaving me and his property in the possession of my stepmother and my guardian. It was in deference to their urgent advice that I left my home in London (with little reluctance, since my life there had never been happy) to study the art of money-making. On arriving at the scene of my expected triumphs I was assigned to the somewhat humble position of errand boy. In common with other boys who performed a like service for the firm I was known as "a pair of legs." Lodgings of a rather modest character had been secured for me in the western outskirts of the city near the banks of the Mersey. I was slow to make friends, and my evenings were spent in the perusal of some story books, which I had brought with me from London. One night, not long after the beginning of my new life in Liverpool, I was lying in bed listening to the wind and rain beating over the housetops and driving against the windows, when suddenly there came a loud rap at my door.

"Who's there?" I demanded, starting out of bed.

As I heard no answer, I repeated my inquiry and stood a

moment listening. I could hear nothing, however, but the wind and rain. Lighting a candle and dressing myself with all haste, I opened the door. I could just discern the figure of a bent old man standing in the hallway, when a gust of wind suddenly put out the candle. The door leading to the street was open, and the old man was probably a straggler come to importune me for shelter or for something to eat. As I relit the candle, he entered my room and stood facing me, but he did not speak. His clothes were dripping and he was blinking at me with strange, gleaming eyes. His hair was snow-white, and as I looked into his face the deathly pallor of it frightened me. His general appearance was more than startling; it was uncanny.

"What can I do for you?" I asked.

Greatly to my surprise he made no reply, but with a look of pain and great anxiety sank into a chair. Then he withdrew from his pocket a letter which he extended to me. The envelope was wet and dirty. It was directed to Kendric Lane, Esq., No. Old Broad street, London, England. The address was crossed and "22 Kirkland street, Liverpool," written under it in the familiar hand of my guardian. A strange proceeding! thought I. Was the letter intended for my father, who was long dead, and who had removed from that address more than ten years ago? The old man began to grin and nod as I examined the superscription. I broke the seal on the envelope and found the following letter, undated, and with no indication of the place from which it was sent:

"Dear Brother - I need your help. Come to me at once if you can. Consequences of vast importance to me and to mankind depend upon your prompt compliance. I cannot tell you where I am. The bearer will bring you to me. Follow him and ask no questions. Moreover, be silent, like him, regarding the subject of this letter. If you can come, procure passage in the first steamer for New York. My messenger is provided with funds. Your loving brother,

"Revis Lane."

I had often heard my father speak of my uncle Revis, who went to America almost twenty years before I was born. Now he was my nearest living relative. No news of him had reached us for many years before my father died. I was familiar with his handwriting and the specimen before me was either genuine, or remarkably like it. If genuine he had evidently not heard of my father's death.

Extraordinary as the message was, the messenger was more so. He sat peering at me with a strange, half-crazed expression on his face.

"When did you leave my uncle?" I asked.

He sat as if unconscious that I had spoken.

I drew my chair to his side and repeated the words in a loud voice, but he did not seem to hear me. Evidently the old man could neither hear nor speak. In a moment he began groping in his pockets, and presently handed me a card which contained the following words:

"If you can come, tear this card in halves and return the right half to him."

I examined the card carefully. The words were

undoubtedly in my uncle's handwriting. The back of the card was covered with strange characters in red ink. I tore the card as directed and handed him the right half.

He held it up to the light and examined it carefully, then put it away in a pocket of his waistcoat. The look of pain returned to his face, and he coughed feebly as if suffering from a severe cold. The hour being late I intimated by pantomime that I desired him to occupy my bed. He understood me readily enough and began feebly to remove his clothing, while I prepared a sofa for myself. He was soon sound asleep, but I lay awake long after the light was extinguished. He was evidently quite ill, and I determined to go for a physician at the first appearance of daylight. As soon as possible I would go with him to my uncle. There were no ties to detain me, and it was clearly my duty to do so. Perhaps my uncle was in some great peril. If so, I might be of service to him.

When I arose in the morning my strange lodger seemed to be sleeping quietly. His face looked pale and ghastly in the light of day. I stepped close to his bed and, laying my hand upon his brow, was horrified to discover that he was dead. What was I to do? I sat down to think, trembling with fright. I must call in a policeman and tell him all I knew about my strange visitor. No, not all; I must not tell him about the letter, thought I. My uncle might not wish it to be published to the world. I ran out upon the street and told the first officer I met how the old man had rapped at my door during the storm; how I had given him my bed out of pity, and how I had discovered on awaking in the morning that he was dead.

That day the body was taken to the morgue. The sum of L100 were found in his pockets, a part of which gave him a decent burial. But while he had gone to his long rest, he had sown in my mind the seed of unrest. I went about my work clinging to the thread of a mystery half told. Whither would it lead me?

Strange as that messenger had seemed, he was certainly a good man to carry secrets.

CHAPTER II

The multitude of legs, engaged by the pair in the service of Valentine, King & Co., were distinguished from each other by a bit of house slang. I was known as "last legs" among my companions for some time after my initiation to the warehouse. At first I was inclined to resent the reduction of my individuality to such a vulgar formula, but as I became inured to hard tasks the sharpness of this indignity wore away.

There was one pair of legs doing service for the firm whose owner became my most valued friend and confidant. In his business capacity he was called "long legs," but his proper name was Philbert Chaffin. He was a tall, slim boy, with blue eyes and light hair, the son of a stage carpenter, who was employed at one of the cheap theatres and who lived within a stone's throw of my lodgings. His language was a unique combination of bad grammar and provincial brogue; but every boy in the warehouse allowed that he was a good fellow. He had spent many an evening with me, and confided to me many a secret which, owing to solemn pledges made at that time, I am not at liberty to divulge, before he invited me to dine and spend an evening with the family. I accepted his invitation gratefully, and the next evening Phil took me over. It was a hearty welcome that I received at the home of the Chaffins. My enjoyment of their simple hospitality would have been perfect but for the embarrassment I felt at the many apologies with which it was offered. Mrs. Chaffin knew as 'ow the tea was not as good as I was used to drinking, but she 'oped it didn't taste "murky." I assured her that it did not taste murky, although a little doubtful as to the exact significance of the word when applied to tea. But in spite of my declaration she insisted that it must taste "murky" to one who was accustomed to better things. The ham was never too good in Liverpool, but she 'oped that it wasn't "reesty." I solemnly declared that it was not "reesty." But Mrs. Chaffin and Mr. Chaffin out of the goodness of their hearts continued to condole with me on the score that such ham tasted and must taste "reesty" to one not used to it. I had no sooner satisfied their misgivings concerning the ham than I was compelled to take issue with them as to the bread, regarding which they entertained a lurking suspicion of staleness. During all of this discussion about the ham, the tea and the bread, I was conscious that a pair of big brown eyes, darkly shaded with long lashes, were staring at me across the table. Whenever I had the courage to glance that way I observed that they had been looking at me intently, and were suddenly averted. These wondering eyes belonged to the only daughter in the family.

"They've all been boys," said Mrs. Chaffin, "since Hetty was born."

I thought it strange that the H in her daughter's name was the only one that the good woman had shown the ability to manage.

"Hetty is the only one of the lot that takes to books," she continued. "The head master told me she will make a good scholar, and dear a me! she does nothing but read books from mornin' till night." While Hetty and her mother removed the dishes we drew our chairs about the fire, and Mr. Chaffin, a blunt, simple-minded man, entertained me with sage observations regarding politics and the weather. He spoke rather loudly, and in a key which, as I learned afterward, he only employed on very special occasions. Presently the youngest lad in the family, who sat on his father's knee, demanded a song. The response was prompt and generous. The selection with which Mr. Chaffin favored us contained upward of forty stanzas, relating the unhappy story of a fair maid and a bold sailor, both of whom met a tragic death, in the last stanza, just before the day set for their marriage. The song being finished, Hetty and her mother drew their chairs up to the fire; Hetty sat next me, and after a severe inward struggle I summoned the courage to ask her a question. She answered me in the fewest words possible, but in a voice so sweet and low that I wondered then and often afterward at its contrast to the other voices I had heard in that house. She wore a home-spun frock and a neat white pinafore, set off with a dainty ribbon tied about her throat.

"She's uncommon still when strangers is here, sir," said Mrs. Chaffin; "but law me! she goes rompitin' about the house like as if she was crazy sometimes, ticklin' her father and tryin' t' snip off his beard with the scissors."

That night was the beginning of happier days for me. When at last I rose to go it was near midnight. I forgot my weariness as I walked to my lodgings, thinking of those simple, honest people and of their kindness to me.

I enjoyed high jinks at the house of the Chaffins at least once a week during the next year of my apprenticeship, near the close of which I began to get ready for a visit to my stepmother in fulfilment of a promise I had made by letter. It had been, on the whole, a happy year to me. I had known many lonely hours, to be sure, but those visits to the little old weather-stained house, in which I found my first friends after leaving home, cheered me from week to week. I knew, too, that Hetty enjoyed those long evenings as much as I did, which meant more to me than I would have dared confess to her. I thought of her a good deal, but it always resulted in the wretched feeling that we were both very young after all. It is not likely that I would have decided to go home for a fortnight, but that I thought it would be pleasant to observe the effect of saying good-by to Hetty. I had no doubt that she would be quite overcome with grief and loneliness after I had gone, and, reckless youth that I was, nothing could have made me more happy than to have known that she really felt grieved on my account. And yet when I called to bid them all good-by, the evening before I started, she betrayed no sign of regret. In fact, she seemed so much happier than usual that I worried about it for weeks, even after I had gone so far away that it seemed doubtful whether we would ever meet again. It did not occur to me that I had been less skilful than she in concealing my emotions, and that she might be merry only because she could perceive that I was sad. Mrs. Chaffin was the only member of the family who seemed to entertain feelings as serious as my own. She had dreamed that I would not come back again, and we all laughed at her then, but when the swift years had revealed some of their secrets, we thought of this prophetic dream with a sadness deeper than any that comes to childish hearts. Hester and Phil walked with me to the gate when I left the house. The radiance of a full moon fell on our faces through the flying clouds. Phil, stupid fellow! had so much to say that I did not get a chance to speak to his sister before she darted back to the house as if pursued. On reaching my lodgings I was surprised to find a gentleman waiting for me.

"Don't know me, eh?" said he, shaking my hand warmly.

He was a tall, portly man, with a kindly face, clean shaven except for a pair of close-cropped, iron-gray side whiskers. I was sure I had seen him before, but couldn't think of his name.

"Earl," said he, handing me a card on which his name and address were printed as follows:

DAVID GORDON EARL,
Barrister at Law,
Lincoln's Inn, London.

I remembered distinctly having accompanied my father to his office on one occasion some years before.

"I've come up from London on purpose to see you. Just got here only a few minutes ago," said he, laying off his overcoat. "But upon my word!" he added, surveying me from head to foot, "I didn't expect to find such a big, strapping fellow as you are. Your surroundings are quite as I had supposed they would be. Cramped quarters in a miserable tumble-down back street! I suppose your guardian provided this place for you?"

"I believe so," said I.

"Did you know that your stepmother had married again?" he asked.

"Married!" I exclaimed. "To whom?"

"To Martin Cobb."

"To my guardian?" I asked, in astonishment.

Not heeding my question, he continued:

"You're intending to go home to-morrow, I believe?"

"Yes, sir."

"My boy," said he, "I have an interest in you. I was your father's friend and adviser for many years. I came all this distance to tell you not to go to London. Do not ask me why, I beg you," said he, with an impatient gesture when I attempted to speak. "It would do you no good to learn my reason for making this request. Listen to this - it's important to you: There's an uncle of yours in America, your nearest relative, I believe. Of course you have heard your father speak of him. A most eccentric fellow! but a man of fine ability. He was a graduate of Oxford and a physician of great skill and learning. Thirty-five years ago he went to Canada and finally settled in a large town on one of the great lakes not far from the border. It was Detroit, I believe. Your father told me, shortly before his death, that he had not heard from your uncle for many years. I have written to him twice within a twelvemonth, but have received no reply. I want you to go over and look him up. If you should find that he is dead, there's no harm done, and you can take time to look about for a business opportunity. If you don't like it, come back, but, if you can content yourself there for awhile, you had better do so."

"But, sir, I have no money."

"You are going for me; I shall, therefore, insist upon

paying the bills. In the success of the undertaking I have, perhaps, as great an interest as you."

"When do you wish me to start?" I asked.

"To-night. That is to say, I would like you to leave this place at once, go with me to a hotel, and sail by the first steamer that leaves for New York."

Ever since that strange and silent messenger had come to me with my uncle's letter I had been haunted by a desire to go in quest of him. Now that it was possible, I hesitated. What would Hester say on hearing that I had gone to America? It would be very grand to write her from New York that I had been suddenly called abroad on important business. Would she care? Of course she would care, and I was willing to wager a sixpence with myself that she would cry bitterly, too, on receiving the letter. Ah, what a punishment that would be for her coldness and indifference!

Yes, I would go. I began picking up my things and packing them into my box.

"I conclude that you have decided to go," he said.

"Yes, sir. I shall be ready in a moment," I replied.

We were soon rattling over the pavements in a cab that had been waiting at the door.

On arriving at the Northwestern Hotel we were informed that a steamer would leave for New York at five in the morning. We drove at once to the dock and having succeeded in making comfortable arrangements for my passage Mr. Earl went aboard the steamer with me. In a retired corner of the great cabin I confessed to him that there was a girl in Liverpool for whom I had a feeling of extraordinary tenderness.

He laughed heartily and insisted that I should tell him all the particulars.

"You are rather young yet to entertain so serious a passion," said he, as he held my hand for a moment before going ashore. "You will get over it as easily as you got into it."

I sat down, unable to reply or to restrain the tears that came to my eyes as he left me alone. I went to my stateroom at once and to bed. What thoughts came to me as I lay there inviting sleep to turn them into dreams, while the great ship waited for the tide! I tossed about my berth; I prayed; I listened. At length I thought I heard my father's voice mingled with others, and a sound of casting off - but I heard no more.

CHAPTER III

One morning in early October, nearly two years after I left Liverpool that memorable night, I found myself in the little city of Ogdensburg, N. Y., past which the majestic St. Lawrence flows with a sleepy movement quite in harmony with the spirit of the old town on its southern shore. All this time I had been vainly beating about the Western Hemisphere in quest of my uncle. He had left Detroit many years before, but I chanced to meet a number of men there who had known him well. Although he had enjoyed a very large practice and a wide reputation for skill, he had made no friends that I could find. He was a man of few words, they told me, and was never seen about the city except in the discharge of his professional duties. Various and conflicting opinions were expressed as to whither he had gone, in testing which I had visited no less than twenty cities, making careful inquiries, especially among medical men. Occasionally I struck what seemed to be a promising clew, which only increased my confusion and left me more hopelessly in the dark. I had reported my movements to Mr. Earl as often as once a week and I received letters from him frequently, encouraging me to continue the search and enclosing money with which to do so. But although I had written often to Hester Chaffin no word from her ever reached me. I was tired of this fruitless quest among strangers, so far from the little that I held dear, and I was on the point of giving up when this paragraph fell under my eye in a Montreal newspaper:

A MYSTERIOUS CHARACTER.

"One who has ever passed the city of Ogdensburg by steamer will no doubt recall a large gambrel-roofed house standing near the water's edge, just out of the town, surrounded by towering trees and enclosed on all sides by a wall nearly as high as the eaves of the building. The wall suggests an asylum, a house of detention or some like place set apart for the unfortunate members of society. In reality, however, it is the residence of a mysterious recluse of the name of Lane, who shut himself up there nearly eighteen years ago and has since been rarely seen. It was built after his own plans, they say, when he came to Ogdensburg with his wife, who died soon afterward. Nobody knows whence he came or anything of his past history. He is apparently a total stranger here below, holding no intercourse with the world beyond that enclosure. His wife is said to have been a woman of great beauty, and her death doubtless threw him into a morbid state of mind, from which he has never rallied. Many years ago he is known to have bought a full-grown African lion from a traveling menagerie, and, soon after, he erected the wall, presumably out of regard for the public safety. Passers along the street have caught an occasional glimpse of him through the high gate, walking in the grounds surrounding his house, with the lion at his heels apparently in complete subjection to its master. A dense thicket runs along the wall on all sides within the enclosure, which, according to local tradition, is alive with rattlesnakes, bred for some strange purpose known only to himself - perhaps to make his isolation more secure.

"He is supposed to have resigned the companionship of men for study and scientific research. He has no children, and his only servant being a deaf-mute, who is almost an idiot, there is little chance at present of learning anything of his life. For more than two years nothing has been seen of the mysterious master of the house. His disappearance would, we think, be a legitimate subject of investigation by the authorities of the town. May he not have been eaten by the lion, or killed by the rattlesnakes? Who knows?"

My heart was beating fast and my hands shook as if stricken with palsy before I had finished the paragraph. The strange old man who had come to me in Liverpool that night was probably the mute servant to which the article referred. In an hour I was on the way to Ogdensburg, quite confident that the issue of my wanderings was at hand. I reached that town next morning nearly two years, as I have said, after the beginning of my journey to the New World. Not stopping to breakfast even, I started out to find the house, which my busy imagination had already pictured for itself. The first townsman I saw directed me to the place.

"Follow the turnpike," said he. "'Sa mild or more - straight ahead. You'll know it when y' git there. 'S' queer place an' stan's off by itself."

The man was going my way, evidently to begin his day's work, for it was then early in the morning, and I walked along with him.

"Folks say," he continued, "them grounds is full of hejious reptyles, an' I've heerd fellers tell queer things they've seen when passin' there at night - red lights a-flyin' about an' spooks at the winders. An' one night, when Uncle Bill Jemson was comin' down the turnpike, they was a storm come up, an' jest as he got opposite the big iron gate they was a flash a lightnin' - an' Bill says he see the ole man, his long white hair a-flyin' in th' wind, an' a lion standin' there in front a th' house. Th' flash was out'n a minit, an' Bill whipped up his hosses an' sent em clear to Mills' tavern on the dead run," said he, laughing as if it were a good joke.

"They don't nobody like th' place ner th' man, though I don' know why, fer no one's ever passed a word with him in these parts. There 'tis, over yender with the pines around it an' th' high wall," said he, pointing with his finger. But my eye had already discovered the low-built rambling house on the high banks of the river, well in the distance, and had recognized it at once.

Leaving my companion at the next turn in the road I walked hurriedly on, and when I had reached the big iron gate I stopped and peered through it. A gravel roadway, now overgrown with weeds, led from the gate to the front of the house, which stood facing me. It was built entirely of wood and consisted of four wings (at least there were no others visible) evidently enclosing a quadrangular courtyard, the rear wings being lower than those in front, and hidden by the latter from the view of one standing at the gate as I was. It was only at a distance that one could see their roofs above the enclosure. There was but one line of windows along the front, but there was an oriel just under the peak of the main building, and I could see a skylight here and there upon the roofs.

The blinds were closed and there was no sign of life about the house - evidently planned with hospitable intentions, but now silent and forbidding. I tried the gates. They were locked securely. A screen of closely woven wire rose from the pavement half way up the iron work. Evidently it would be impossible to reach the doors without scaling this barrier, and I was not yet ready to try an expedient so desperate. Returning to my hotel I wrote a letter to the master of the house, telling him of my long-continued quest and of my hopes regarding our possible kinship. Day after day I anxiously awaited his reply, until a week had passed, but no word came from him. In passing the house at different times, however, I observed some signs of life within it - a blind open that had been closed the day before - a faint glimmer of light on the trees in the rear of the grounds at night, which might have come from the back windows. Even this slight encouragement was gratifying, but as time passed without bringing any reply to my letter I began to think that, after all, my hopes rested on very shadowy foundations. One day I asked the local postmaster if a man of the name of Lane, who lived near that city, ever sent for his mail.

"Never," said he. "The man is crazy, I guess, and it's wasting postage to write him. He's a hermit, sir - a regular hermit, and is about the same as dead, for nobody ever sees him. The tradesmen tell me that his old servant comes out of an evening, once in a while, to buy provisions, but he's deaf as a post and dumb as an oyster." The interview had at least shown me the futility of trying to reach him by letter.

It was clear that only one course was open to me. I must brave the unknown perils with which this strange man had encompassed the path of the trespasser, and gain an entrance to the house. I sought the seclusion of my room at once, and thought over the result of my investigations. I had not written to my good friend in London since my arrival in Ogdensburg, and I concluded not to do so until I could give him definite information.

Late in the afternoon a slow, drizzling rain began to pour down, and when night fell every luminary in the heavens was obscured by thick clouds. It was a favorable time for carrying out my project, as the darkness was intensified by a fog that had settled over the city. By the light of my lamp I prepared for the undertaking, in such a state of excitement that I was frequently startled by my own whispers, through which I found myself now and then giving involuntary utterance to my thoughts. Cutting up a pair of boots which I carried in my box, I wound my legs in leather from my ankles up above my knees, carefully drawing on a pair of thick, long stockings to hold it in place. This precaution would give me a comfortable sense of security, even if there were no snakes to fear. I felt sure that the lion, if he were still living, would be kept in some place of confinement.

It was long past bedtime, and the lights were out in every shop and dwelling, when I started on my daring mission. The little lamps that glared through the fog at the street corners could scarcely be seen twenty feet away. I was so preoccupied that I frequently lost my direction in the mud and darkness. It seemed as if I had been traveling for hours, when at last I felt the big wall, and saw its dim bulk rising above me and stretching away into the night. Cautiouly I groped along its base until my hands felt the iron bars of the gate. Then I stood for some moments leaning against them, quite out of breath. They were cold and wet, and chilled me to a shiver when I touched them. I peered toward the house but could see nothing. I listened, but could hear nothing except the beating of my own heart and the mournful sound of the pines whose loftier branches were stirring in the still air. Grasping the heavy bars I tried to climb the gate, but, as there were no projections on which it was possible to get a foothold, I found this an exhausting and difficult task. I climbed repeatedly several feet above the earth, only to lose my foothold and slide down again. Finally, by exerting all my strength, I succeeded in supporting myself with the edge of my boot upon a crossbar about half way up; then, taking a small rope from my pocket I threw one end of it over the gate, holding the other in my teeth. Tying it securely by a noose I climbed hand over hand to the top and then let myself down on the other side. I was quite exhausted by the effort (unaccustomed as I was to such burglarious enterprises) and my fingers were torn and bleeding from forcing a hold between the iron work and the wire screen. I remembered the gravel pathway, overgrown with grass, that led from the big gate to a front door. I groped about in the darkness until I felt the gravel under my feet. Then I moved cautiously along it, until I could dimly discern the outlines of the house. My nerves were so wrought up, while I stood there holding my breath to catch some sound from its gloomy interior, that I was near crying out in abject terror at every step. An owl, startled from the limb of a tree over my head, flew lazily into the upper air and across the thicket, disturbing other birds that set up a chattering protest. Stealthily I crept from window to window, but the blinds were closed fast. Finally I came to a door that seemed to open into the main part of the building. Desperate under the strain to which my nerves had been subjected, I knocked loudly on its upper panels. The sound echoed through the still house and the thickly wooded grounds around it. "God help me!" I whispered; "will that echo never cease?" It kept repeating itself from tree to tree, until I covered my ears to stop its weird reverberations. Then I heard a low threatening sound, deep and resonant as the lower tones of a great organ, that gradually grew louder until its volume filled the air, and then died away, while its echoes went chasing each other among the trees. In the silence which followed, my ear caught another sound the like of which I had never heard before. A dozen clocks being wound by quick turns on all sides of me would, I fancy, have produced a similar effect. It was evident to me that my knocking had disturbed my uncle's pets, but I was not to be frightened away. Hearing no movement in the house I tried the door, and to my astonishment it swung open. A peculiar odor, such as one notices in a house that has long stood empty, came to my nostrils, and again I heard that fateful whirring, but in the darkness I could discern no object. As I crossed the threshold the sound grew louder, and to my horror the door closed suddenly behind me. Hurriedly striking a match, I held it above my head and peered about me. Its light revealed a small apartment finished in polished wood. Along the angle of the floor was an opening, two or three inches high, into the side walls. And half way up the wall in front of me I saw a face - the face of a maniac it seemed to be - pale and wan, with strange, inhuman eyes. I had scarcely glanced at it when the match dropped from my fingers and fell slowly through the air, going out as it struck the floor. My hands were cold, but so wet with perspiration that they stuck to my clothing when I felt for a candle which I had brought with me.

There are moments in every man's life that move slowly, as if carrying the weight of years upon their backs. I shall never cease to believe that the few seconds it took me to light that candle must stand for as many years in any correct reckoning of my age. When its beams at last illumined the room, the strange face was still there. Had I seen it before? It was marvellously like that other face which had haunted my dreams so long. If it was the face of a man he must be standing on the other side of the wall and looking through a panel.

"Is Mr. Lane at home?" I asked in an unnatural tone that startled me.

But no word of reply was spoken.

"I am his nephew and I have important news for him."

The face disappeared for a moment, and presently a shrunken hand, holding a white sheet of paper, was extended through the opening. I stepped forward, took the sheet and, withdrawing to the centre of the room, sat down upon the floor and wrote the following message in bold characters with my pencil:

"Kendric Lane, son of Kendric Lane (deceased), late of London, England, wishes to see Dr. Lane on business of importance."

I handed the message to the strange man behind the wall, who immediately disappeared with it, closing the panel. "The worst is over," thought I, while I stood in that mysterious and silent chamber waiting for his return. But I should not have thought so had I known what was still to be revealed to me before the dawn of another day, and in the months that followed, during which that house and its echoing groves were my home. And I sometimes ask myself, in the light of later events of which that visit was indirectly the cause, whether, had I been able to foresee them, I would still have persevered in my purpose to know the secrets of my uncle's house?

CHAPTER IV

A long time I stood waiting for some reply to my message. My candle was fast burning out, and I began to fear that after all I was likely to leave the house no wiser than when I had entered it. Suddenly a door swung on its creaking hinges and a feeble old man, holding a lamp in one hand, stood grinning at me in the opening. It was the same face that I saw before, but it seemed less ghostly and unnatural now. Stepping back he beckoned me to enter. As soon as I had crossed the threshold the door closed behind me and the old man carefully bolted it. I stood in a large room, richly furnished, of which spiders had apparently long held possession. Great cobwebs hung like hammocks from the ceiling, and the dust of years had settled over all. Two human skeletons completely wrapped in cobwebs, stood facing me against the opposite wall. Following my silent leader, I went through a long narrow passage, at the end of which was a heavy door fastened with large iron bolts. Before opening it the strange old man placed the lamp upon a table and turning around looked squarely into my face. Merciful Heaven! It was the face of another man who was looking at me now! The deep lines had almost disappeared and the eyes looked brighter and more intelligent. No, it was the same face, for while my eyes were eagerly scanning it that hideous grin began to deepen its wrinkles, and its owner, taking half a dozen steps down the passageway, made an awkward motion with both hands as if trying to indicate that I was to follow him very closely. Then he opened the big door and I was surprised to observe that it led into the outer air. What gulf of darkness are we about to plunge into? I asked myself, peering through the doorway; and as we stepped out I heard again that ominous whirring. Close upon his heels I followed in a narrow path, through what seemed to be a large court-yard, overgrown with thick grass. Presently he stopped, and, taking a bunch of keys from his pocket, unlocked a door in a back wing of the house. Reaching out until his hand touched me, as if to make sure that I was there, he swung the door open and we stepped into a dimly lighted apartment. My mysterious guide turned up the wick of a lamp that was burning on a table in the centre of the room. It was a library, with great shelves of books reaching from floor to ceiling along its walls. A large galvanic battery, globes, charts and other contrivances that belong to the equipment of a scholar surrounded the table. This table was used for writing evidently, for there were pens lying on it and a human skull used as an inkstand, the fluid being held in the cavities of the eyes. I had seated myself in a chair and was waiting for some sign from the little old man who had brought me there. But where was he? Turning around I looked about me on all sides. He had left the room during my momentary preoccupation. I had scarcely seated myself again when a door opened and a venerable man, with snow-white hair and a smooth-shaven face that was pale and wrinkled, walked slowly toward me. I rose to my feet and advanced a step or two. He came forward without speaking and looked steadily into my eyes. Slowly and sadly he turned his gaze upon the floor, apparently in deep thought. A sigh broke from his lips as if some memory, stirring in the caves of thought, had driven it forth.

The man who stood before me had deep-set gray eyes, almost concealed by long shaggy brows not yet entirely white. His lips were thin, and drawn closely together above a square, protruding chin. The nose was aquiline and prominent, with large, but finely cut nostrils. Altogether his was the most picturesque face I had ever seen. Suddenly he made an effort to clear his throat.

"Kendric's child," said he, in a strange, low voice. He spoke slowly and with great difficulty, as if his organs of speech were partially paralyzed. I would not have been able to distinguish his words but for the silence of that room and the unnatural keenness of my hearing. He still stood motionless, his eyes upon the floor. I knew that he was thinking of my father.

"Dead?" he asked, looking at me inquisitively.

"He is dead," I answered.

"And my man - did he give you the letter?"

"Yes; he is dead also."

"Dead? I thought he was dead," he repeated, slowly and thoughtfully. "I, too, am dead - long dead."

The words were separated by considerable pauses, and he faced me almost sternly as he finished speaking them. I stood staring at him, dumb with surprise.

"Why - how did you come here?"

He sank into a chair, exhausted with the effort it had cost him to speak. My presence seemed to irritate and annoy him. Why, indeed, had I come there? What should I say in reply to his question? I tried to think.

"Knaves! Knaves!" said my uncle, in a shrill voice, rushing toward me. In a moment he had thrown his arms about my neck and was sobbing aloud. My heart was full and I wept with him.

"Fortunate child of God," said he, after a moment; "you have the seed of life - immortal life. But I beg you to go. To one like you this house will seem an uncanny place; I can only think of it as beyond the grave."

"Let me stay, uncle," said I. "Don't send me away. Perhaps I can help you or comfort you."

"Poor soul! you shall stay if you will. I am in great trouble and need help, but you are a boy - I cannot ask you to give your life to me."

He sat down before the table, breathing heavily, and beckoned me to a chair beside him. I was quite dumfounded and knew not what to say. Presently he began writing upon large sheets of paper, handing each one to me as soon as it was covered. The manuscript read as follows:

"I am not able to talk much. To me words are a lie and an abomination. Even these I now write are misrepresenting me and deceiving you, though I wish them to tell the truth. They will make me out an ass or a madman. I am neither. For eighteen years I have scarcely spoken as many words. A word or two of Sanscrit now and then has met my needs, thank God! There is an interior language for which speech is an imperfect medium. Through that interior language thought is communicated directly and truthfully. I used it long before I came here - imperfectly, to be sure, but with a small degree of satisfaction to myself. Through it I was able to heal the sick when others failed. I knew how they felt better than they could tell me in feeble words. In some more perfect state of evolution, beyond the grave, perhaps, all men will have this power and it will be perfect. I can enjoy but an imperfect use of it until the mortal part of me has been cast off. One trained to speech in childhood loses certain faculties that can never be regained.

"My wife died many years ago. She left me a broken heart and a child, newly born. I had just built this house, among strangers. We intended to devote the remainder of our lives to the study of mental phenomena. We desired to carry on our work without interruption. We planned to live unknown among those around us. When she died I saw in the child an opportunity. I determined to make its life a grand experiment; to preserve and cultivate its native intuitions - the germ of the power of direct communication. God has vouchsafed success to me. He lives - a man of exalted powers the like of which the world has never seen but once, and then in Christ, the very Son of God. But, unlike Him, my son is only human, with weaknesses that are our common lot.

"The years are flying, and strength is failing! I must die soon and he will live. That thought burns my brain, passing through it day by day. His life may be long extended and he cannot live alone, nor among men, for he would be a stranger and friendless - feared and dreaded by superstitious fools. He has never seen a human face outside these walls nor heard a human voice but mine. I have told you my trouble."

He ceased writing, but before I had finished reading the

statement some strange influence came over me. I felt restless and uncomfortable. My hand was shaking so that I could scarcely read the words on the last sheet of paper. Suddenly I raised my eyes and saw a young man, godlike in form and feature, standing at my side. His face wore an expression of indescribable eloquence. As familiar as he afterward became to me, I can never forget the first impression which that magnificent human being made upon my mind, as he stood there - radiating a power that I felt to the tips of my fingers. What favored son of man was this confronting me, born to such an inheritance of majesty and grace? I asked myself, regarding him with amazement. He had eyes dark as night, set under a broad forehead, about which wavy masses of tawny hair fell gracefully. His stately form was erect and firm as a statue. For a moment his eyes looked into mine; then he advanced and took my hand. Tenderly he pressed it to his lips, stepping back as he did so and looking at me with a half-curious, half-amused expression. I was so startled by the unexpected appearance of this remarkable figure that I had not, until now, noticed that a large lion had followed him into the room and was lying quietly at his feet. I was not afraid; indeed, the king of beasts seemed but a part of the man's masterful presence. I do not think I would have seen the animal but that his enormous body was lying directly before my eyes on the floor. My uncle had been sitting with his head resting upon his hand at the table. Suddenly he rose and a strange, guttural sound - it may have been a word from some language wholly unfamiliar to me - passed his lips. The young man immediately left us, the lion following closely at his heels. We both sat in silence for some moments after he had gone. My mind had felt strange exhilaration in his presence, and I rubbed my eyes to make sure that I was not dreaming. When I looked at my uncle the sad expression on his face had given way to a smile of infinite satisfaction.

"He is pleased - thank God!" said my uncle, in a hoarse whisper, sinking into a chair.

I made no answer.

"It was my son," he continued, with animation. "Rayel - that was the name she gave him. Rayel, the wonderful. He will love you as he loves me. Come," said he, rising, "the night is nearly gone."

Taking a lamp from the table, he beckoned me to follow him. Silently we proceeded through a narrow hallway and up one flight of stairs to a spacious bedroom which had seemingly been prepared for my use. A candle was burning dimly on a large dressing-case, and by its flickering light, as soon as my uncle had gone, I looked about me and tried to think with calmness on the experience I had passed through. Bolting the door securely, I threw open one of the window blinds. To my surprise the first light of dawn was visible in the sky. My room was in the rear of the house. Between me and the high wall was a dense tangle of underbrush, barely visible in the dim light. Hastily undressing, I went to bed without further delay, and was soon in deep sleep. When I awoke it was near midday. Dressing as quickly as possible, I proceeded at once to the library, where my uncle sat waiting for me. He conducted me to the breakfast room - a well-lighted and cheerful apartment - where he served me with his own hands.

"You shall stay, sir - you shall stay," said he, laying his hand on my shoulder as he sat down beside me, with a smiling face. "Rayel loves you. He hopes you will stay. He thinks God sent you to us."

"I am glad, for I wish to stay," I said.

"Good!" he exclaimed, in a long whisper. "You have brought the world to him. Already he has seen it in your eyes. But it is good!"

While I ate he asked me questions touching the changes in our family since he left England.

I told him of my life at home after my father's death; of my hard lot in Liverpool, and of the midnight interviews with his messenger and with Mr. Earl. He listened to me with grave and attentive interest, but stopped me before I had finished, with an impatient gesture.

"Speak out! they meant - they meant to kill you, didn't they?"

I stared at him in amazement, while ideas that were new to me flocked into the empyrean of thought like black birds of prey. Oh, no; I had never suspected that! I would never before have permitted such a hideous suspicion to enter my mind. Was it possible that Mr. Earl had sent me away from England in order to save my life? My hands began to tremble, and I felt my face turning red and pale under the searching eyes of my uncle.

"My boy," said he, "if all the murders were done that men conceive, the devil would live alone on earth. We shall know some time - I tell you we shall know! Let us go to Rayel," he said, rising and leading the way.

The interview had greatly excited him, and his speech seemed even more halting and labored than before. Many of his words were mispronounced and separated by long pauses; but his manner was marvelously expressive, and often a peculiar turn of the eye or movement of the hand made his meaning clear when I was in doubt about his words.

I followed him through a long gymnasium and out upon a grassy courtyard extending along the rear of the grounds parallel with the river wall for a hundred yards or more, and adorned with beds of flowers. It was completely shut off from the eye of the outside world by a thick grove and an impenetrable growth of underbrush that reached beyond the lowest branches of the trees. Nothing but the blue sky, in which the sun was on its downward course, the house, and the walls of living green, were visible. Out of this Eden-like spot we passed into another wing of the building with large windows looking out upon it. Rayel met us at the door, dressed in a black robe of silk that hung gracefully from his shoulders. Again he took my hand and kissed it, then looked into my eyes with the same expression of curious interest upon his face that I had noted before. Still holding my hand, he led me across the room. For the first time I noticed that its walls were covered with pictures, unframed, and that an easel stood in the light of each window. We stopped before one of them. On a large canvas that was stretched across it I saw a likeness of myself. The eyes wore a haggard look which seemed unnatural. But there was something strangely real about it, in spite of that.

"Wonderful!" said I.

Rayel started at the sound of my voice, and glanced from one to the other with a puzzled, inquiring look. Turning to his father, he uttered some strange monosyllable in a deep voice. Then he took my hand and walked back and forth across the room with me, smiling in great delight. I was fascinated by one of the pictures which showed a great gleaming eye with a suggestion of lightning in its fiery depths, as if taken at the keenest flash of fury. To intensify its fierceness a human hand was raised in front of it so as to throw a dark shadow across the canvas.

"It is the lion's eye," said my uncle, who was standing near me.

There were other paintings - many of them equally strange and wonderful - hanging on the walls, some of which contained material he could not have derived from direct observation. It was easy to discern in his work the fragments of nature that came within the limited command of his own eyes - the falling snow, the changing phases of the sky and of vegetation - for they were presented with a stronger and more vivid touch. Until the fading twilight blended all color into gloom I passed from one canvas to another along the wall in silence, oblivious of all save the presence of Rayel, who followed close at my elbow, evidently enjoying my admiration of his work. When I had finished looking at the paintings I turned for some sign to indicate his further pleasure, and discovered that he was gone. My uncle was standing near me.

"It is late," said he.

We returned at once across the yard to my uncle's retreat among his books and papers. Lighting the lamps he sat down beside me.

"The power of speech is returning," said he. "I can talk more easily."

"Did I not hear you speak to your son?" I asked.

"Yes," he answered. "Long ago difficulties arose. Sometimes he could not command my thoughts, nor I his. I had known fifty years of life; he had not - hence an inequality. My physical organism had been neglected. It was an imperfect agent of the mind. Many of my faculties were lost. These circumstances stood between us like barriers. It was the beginning of each communication that troubled us, when our minds were working in different channels. Something was needed for a cue - a starting-point. Ten pregnant words of Sanscrit were all we needed. It was easy then."

"I should think he would have lost the power of speech and hearing," I remarked.

"No. Music saved them - abstract music. His voice is wonderful. His hearing is quick. Rayel knows words but not speech. His mind has command of my knowledge. He has never seen the world, but he knows about it. I tried to begin my life anew and to forget the past. But I could not wholly cleanse my mind of it. Its memories faded slowly. I have avoided renewing them for his sake."

"He could, then, learn to speak?"

"With ease, and it were better if he could speak now. We will teach him soon."

As he ceased speaking, fatigued by the unaccustomed effort, I heard low strains of music echoing through the silent halls around us. A violin! The tone was deep and tremulous, gradually growing louder, filling the ear with its message, and lifting the mind to lofty heights of thought and passion. We both sat listening for hours, and midnight came before the last strain died away. That music was like a strange story that drops its plummet deep into life's mysteries.

"A new song!" said my uncle, turning to me with surprise on his face. "He got the subject from you. We shall see."

Presently Rayel entered the room, bringing something in his hand - a picture - which he held up to the lamplight. A girl's face! and wonderfully like that of Hester Chaffin. I sat amazed, staring at it. But the likeness was not exact, the face was idealized - as I had seen it in my dream the night before. I raised my eyes to Rayel's face. He was looking at me with an expression of pain and embarrassment.

CHAPTER V

My uncle recovered the power of speech rapidly. Before I had been a week in his house he was able to talk with comparative ease. He seemed to enjoy my companionship, and I spent most of my time in his library, conversing with him or conning the musty books that had long lain unread. To me this room was a fascinating and restful place. Somehow it reminded me of an old cemetery. The time-worn books upon its shelves stood in solemn rows, like headstones, sacred to the memory of the men who wrote them - their titles like inscriptions half obliterated. I did not see Rayel for days after the midnight episode that gave me such a startling revelation of his power.

"Do you think that Rayel knows everything that passes in one's mind - a vivid dream, for instance?" I asked my uncle one day when we were alone together.

Yes, except when he is himself asleep. His command of my dreams puzzled me at first. I thought I had put the past completely out of my mind. But I could not hide it from him. Little by little he learned everything in my history. One day I saw him at work on a picture. It startled me. The canvas showed a man lying on a surgeon's table. The knife had just severed an artery in his thigh. There were four men working over him - I was one of them. Gradually the features took on a familiar expression. His face grew paler under the brush. A few touches - the scene was complete. The man was dead - his eyes wide open, staring at me.

My uncle paused and looked earnestly into my face.

"It was a bit of your professional experience," said I. "Something had reminded you of it."

"The night before I dreamed about it" he answered. "My mind, released from the command of my will, betrayed me."

"A strange power!" I exclaimed.

"Incredible to you! Impossible to acquire unless the work begins at birth, and then the possibilities are infinite," said he, drawing his chair closer to mine. "You know what I have done. Start the new-born mind on any highway and see how it hurries along. You can do more, working a little while over the cradle, than all the preachers under heaven, after its occupant has grown beyond your ministry. I tell you, sir, the world is indifferent to its children. Neglected by their parents, subject to hired tenderness or none at all; left to the care of ignorant or depraved nurses, and often taught little but selfishness and greed of gain, the children of men are surrounded by destructive agencies. Can we wonder that the human mind loses in infancy so much of its native power? But so the generations of earth are growing up, bearing embittered fruit and sowing its seed to the four winds. Who cares for the mind and body of a child has the highest possible mission - the most sacred of all trusts. He must give it all his time and strength. He must lead its mind into green pastures; he must share its joys; he must know its hopes and fears; he must give it hold on lines of thought that reach into eternity, which will sooner or later flood it with inspiration; he must see that the brain has a sufficient foundation of flesh and blood and bone; he must give it all his life until the germs of power are developed."

"Unfortunately," said I, "most parents have other things to do and think of."

"Parentage is a crime under such circumstances. It has peopled the world with fools and knaves. It delays the coming of Christ's kingdom. There are a few wise men, but they are held down as gravitation holds the rock. There are laws of attraction in the world of mind as in that of matter. Good and evil are its poles. Every atom between them is held in place by the operation of opposing forces. The general mass of mind lies within narrow zones on both sides of the equatorial line of this imaginary world. Its attraction prevents any men from rising far above or descending far below it. I tell you, sir, the intellectual world has degrees of latitude and longitude which determine every man's location. Emancipated from the forces I have described, my son has risen to a level beyond the attainment of men under ordinary conditions. Hypocrisy and deceit are things of which he knows nothing. I do not ascribe to him, mind you, the possession of saintly virtues. He is a man in whom the best potentialities of mind and body have been developed. I have carefully avoided the danger of making him a morbid, spiritual creature. His body is quite as wonderful as his mind."

My uncle had been pacing restlessly up and down the room as he spoke, often pausing before me and uttering his words vehemently, with quick gestures and flashing eyes. He did not, seemingly, expect an answer to his remark, for, as he ceased speaking, he stepped before one of the windows and stood for a moment looking out upon the courtyard.

"See!" said he suddenly, motioning to me.

I stepped to his side and, looking through the window, saw Rayel running across the lawn with the lion on his shoulders. When the beast sprang down he seized it by the mane and tossed it about like one with the strength of Hercules. Here was a man who exercised his rightful dominion over animated nature!

"The beast is very fond of him," said my uncle, "and a movement of his finger is sufficient to control it."

"Why did you adopt a pet so terrible?" I asked.

"To secure isolation," he answered. "He's an object of terror to intruders, and a source of delight to us."

"You have snakes here, too," I ventured.

"Yes, and for the same reason, But they can't harm you now. Since you came we have killed them. They have been good friends to me, but you were a stranger, and your life would have been in danger every day. Years ago I procured a score of them from the mountains of Pennsylvania and put them into the thickets. They multiplied like rats, and so I was armed against invasion.

"To prevent their escape I sank a screen of wire two feet below the ground along the base of the walls; I also posted a warning inside my gate. Long ago I began to destroy them, and there were only a few left when you came. They were good friends to me - excellent friends!" he repeated, rubbing his hands with a grim smile. "For eighteen years I have been able to carry on my work unmolested. No knowledge of what was transpiring outside this little world has ever reached me."

"How did you begin the work of teaching this interior language to Rayel?" I asked.

"By signs at first - gradually making them more simple and suggestive. The elimination of signs kept pace with the development of his intuitions. It was slow work and hard work, but I gave all my time to it. After he became familiar with a sign, I began to make it less pantomimic, until finally a lift of the eyebrow, a movement of the lips, or an inclination of the head served to express my meaning. In time he could detect the passing shades of expression in my eyes and understand them. Look at me," said he, laying his hand on my head and watching my eyes as the firelight shone upon them, for it was now evening.

"Don't you know, my boy, that your eyes reflect what is passing in your mind? Then there are countless nerves and muscles in your face which proclaim thought. They aid my intuitions to discover what you do not speak. You wonder - ah! you are afraid! - afraid of me."

I started in my chair, for while he was looking into my eyes a strange gleam came into his own. He turned about suddenly and looked into the bright fire that burned on the grate before us.

"Never fear," he continued, nervously twirling a lock of his white hair. "Never fear, sir - I am not mad. Not yet. I have been afraid of it, but my reason will outlast my life. Do you ever pray?"

"Every day," I answered.

"Then you employ the interior language. We commune directly with the Holy Spirit. You get some message from Him every day more satisfactory than words. It's the answer of your prayers. I tell you, sir, words are an invention of the devil. Do you like Rayel?" he asked, turning upon me abruptly.

"You need have no doubt of that," I answered, "or of my willingness to look after him if it should be necessary - to take him away with me and cherish him as I would a brother."

"Good! Good!" he exclaimed smiling and rubbing his hands joyfully. "I have not long to live. When the time comes, take him out among the knaves and fools! But we must hurry: our time is short. We must prepare him for a second birth. You will find him an apt pupil - a very apt one. He already knows more of the world than I thought possible. I don't think you will find him troublesome - he can help you; he will teach you wisdom; he will enlarge the issues of your life. My fortune will be ample for his needs: use it as you see fit. I have one servant left," he said, drawing his chair closer to mine and speaking scarcely above a whisper: "I would like this to be his home when I am dead. It will be better, however, to place him in some public institution where he can be well provided for. I shall leave a sufficient allowance for him. The manner of its bestowal I leave entirely to your judgment. There were two of them - you have seen the other. He was a faithful fellow. They were poor fools, both of them, but uncommonly wise," he continued.

"They kept it to themselves. I found them in an asylum twenty-five years ago. They called them idiots. Idiots! God help us!"

That strange light seemed to kindle in his eyes again while he was speaking, and it conveyed anything but a cheerful suggestion to my mind.

"There is this difference between idiots and madmen," he continued. "The former are born outside the pale of human sympathy; the latter overstep it. In either case they are not of this earth - they are embodied spirits living in a world of their own creation, biding the time of liberation from the flesh. And do you know, there are more madmen in the world than it dreams of?"

He stopped with a tone of sharp interrogation and looked squarely into my face.

"There are undoubtedly many of them," said I.

"The lines of monomania all lead to madness," he continued. "The deeper one plunges into the mysteries of life the nearer he approaches it. But, mark you, one man may venture further than another. For years I have lived in fear of two things - madness and death. Not on my account, but I had Rayel to think of."

My uncle rose to his feet before he had ceased speaking and walked stealthily on his tiptoes to an open door, where he stood for a moment listening. I could hear nothing but the sound of the wind whistling in the chimney.

"Wait here," he whispered presently, and then disappeared through the door, closing it after him. I held my watch down to the firelight and saw it was near eleven o'clock. I felt drowsy, and had almost fallen asleep, when my uncle returned, carrying a lantern. "Rayel is asleep," said he, in a whisper. "Won't you come with me? - it will not take long."

"Certainly," said I, rising, and waiting for him to lead the way. He put on his antique hat and threw a shawl over his shoulders.

"It's a chilly night," said he. "You'd better wear another coat."

I drew on my overcoat at once, wondering what new experience awaited me. Holding the lantern in front of him, he proceeded slowly and feebly across the rear courtyard, and unlocked a door in one of the side wings of the house, through which we passed into a large unfurnished room.

"I always wait till he's asleep," said my uncle, shuffling across the room and unlocking another door on its opposite side. "He's never been here - never yet," he continued, pulling the door open. The dim light of the lantern shone out upon a thicket of fragrant spruce and cedar. As I stepped down upon the ground, following in the steps of my uncle, I could hear the murmur of the great pines towering far above our heads. Slowly we made our way through the dense undergrowth, and soon entered an open space carpeted with pine needles and moss. It was a circular plot in the thicket, and out of its centre rose an immense pine, whose upper branches wholly obscured the sky. My uncle hung his lantern on a knot protruding from the trunk of the tree, and slowly knelt upon the ground, covering his face with his hands. Suddenly he beckoned to me, and I knelt down beside him.

"Listen!" said he. "Do you hear voices? She comes to me here. Can you see her - my wife? Look about you, do you not see her?"

He laid his trembling hand upon my shoulder. Again I saw that awful gleam in his eyes. The gruesome suggestion he had made set my nerves tingling, and I peered about among the shadows of that dimly lighted recess, half expecting some vision to greet my eyes. Then there came a loud rustling of the branches high above us. The lantern light flared up and suddenly went out, leaving us in total darkness.

"She is here!" he whispered, in excitement. "Sit still - do not speak."

A deep silence, intensified by the sound of the night wind in the trees around us, followed my uncle's words. The going out of the light he had seemed to regard as a signal from the spirit world, and I sat still as he bade me, not doubting that his acute senses had penetrated the veil which limited my own vision. I had seen so many revelations of his strange power that I now sat awestruck and afraid, waiting for some word from him to end my suspense. I could see nothing in the darkness, but I could hear my uncle breathing heavily, as if trying to suppress his emotion. Suddenly there was a stir in the bushes near us. Then I heard a step like that of a man on the thickly covered earth close by my side. I stretched out prone upon the ground, covering my face with my hands. I could hear a sound as of some one groping about in the darkness, and then I felt the touch of a strange hand upon my shoulder.

CHAPTER VI

I shrank from the hand that touched me and, moving quickly aside, struck a match and peered around. By its light I could discern the form of a man standing near the edge of the thicket. Rising to my feet I took down the lantern and lighted it. There, standing before me, was the grinning mute who had admitted me to the house. My uncle, who was still kneeling, rose feebly to his feet, his eyes wet with tears.

"Good friend!" said he, taking the lantern from me and handing it to the mute. "He alway comes for me here."

We followed the old servant in silence through the thick boughs of cedar until we came to the door of a low-roofed wooden building that stood by itself in the thicket. The mute opened the door, ushering us into a small room containing a bed and some simple furniture. A comfortable wood fire was burning in a large open stove, and we both sat down in front of it, shivering from exposure to the chilly air of the night. My uncle handed a key to the mute, who unlocked a cupboard, taking from it a decanter of whiskey, which he set before us with glasses.

"It will warm you," said my uncle, pouring out the

spirits: "I have seen my wife. She always comes to me there - when the light goes out. She knows your heart better than I. We shall leave Rayel to your care. It is the last time I shall come here. My work is nearly finished."

We emptied our glasses in silence, but my mind was busy thinking on those impressive words, "She always comes to me there - when the light goes out."

It was strange - this going out of the light just at that moment. Was it not possible, I asked myself, that the lantern, being always hung on the same projection, was thus in the way of a current of air passing down the trunk of the tree when a gust of wind struck its lofty branches? If so, the knot would naturally conduct the current into the opening at the top of the lantern. My reflections were interrupted by my uncle, who rose, and, taking a candle, asked me to accompany him. I followed him into a cellar filled with casks and barrels containing, as I supposed, wine and provisions for future use. Returning, we passed through a large room, in one end of which many boxes and barrels were stored. I afterward learned that there was a large garden and poultry yard in this lonely nook where my uncle's only servant was sequestered.

I was glad when we started back through the thicket, for the hour was late and I felt the need of sleep.

"He gives us our food," said my uncle, when we were at length in the courtyard. "We have enough of everything needful - but little meat. It destroys mental power. It is fools' food."

Next day my uncle was unable to leave his bed. I determined to go to the hotel for my baggage and to post some letters, one of which gave Mr. Earl an account of my experiences since the October night when I became an inmate of that house.

It was midwinter now, and the long stretches of pasturage and meadow land outside the walls were blasted and sere when the old mute, whom I had seen twice before, let me out of the big gate. When I returned he was there to open the gate for me and help me with my baggage.

I found Rayel at his father's bedside. The sick man was asleep, and I went at once to the library, where Rayel soon came, as was his custom in the afternoon, for a lesson in talking. Both my uncle and myself had taken great pains to teach him this accomplishment, and his progress had been even more rapid than we thought possible. He caught the significance of words with astonishing ease, but found some difficulty in producing their sound. He went about it with great patience, however, repeating the hardest words after me until he was able to pronounce them correctly. But although the work was often tedious we both got much fun out of it. I had never heard the sound of laughter in that house. One day I broke its solemn spell by laughing heartily at the grotesque distortion of my cousin's face incidental to the production of a difficult sound. He stopped suddenly and looked at me, half alarmed. This made me laugh more heartily, and he grasped my hand with the serious air of a physician feeling the pulse of his patient. Being assured there was no danger, he indulged in a little offhand cachinnation himself and was, I judged, well pleased with the trial, for he repeated it frequently afterward, and greatly to his amusement.

The word "woman," and others related to it, puzzled

IRVING BACHELLER

him not a little, for he had never seen a woman, except through the medium of my own mind and that of his father. The subject interested him, and he gave much serious thought to it, questioning me closely at some of our interviews, as if dissatisfied with the idea conveyed to him. Our discussions, however, had reached some slumbering chord in him, which, once touched, stirred his blood with its vibrations. I do not think his isolation could have lasted much longer, for he became restless and eager to see the world.

Rayel was greatly depressed by his father's illness. For months after that night, the excitement of which had so hastened the failure of the old man's strength, the silence of the great house was rarely broken by the sound of our voices. My uncle lay helpless in a deep sleep most of the time, never able to leave his bed until, revived by the freshness of approaching summer, he had strength enough to sit in an easy-chair by the window. Some fatal malady, the nature of which he did not disclose to me, was evidently sapping his strength. I had urged him more than once to let me summon a physician, but he would not permit me to do so. When summer came at last, he grew stronger, and was able to walk, supported by Rayel, to his chair in the open courtyard among the flowers.

The lion, which had been confined in its cage most of the time since my uncle had grown so feeble as to need Rayel's constant attention sickened and died in the warm days of early June. Rayel was sorely grieved by the death of his pet, and although he stood in the shadow of a far greater sorrow, he felt deeply the loss of this lifelong friend. The summer passed slowly, one day like another, casting on us the same burden of anxiety and silence. I spent much of the time in my uncle's library, poring over his books and trying to shake off the melancholy thoughts suggested by my daily life.

One day in early autumn, Rayel was sitting with me near an open window overlooking the courtyard, where his father was enjoying the open air.

"He will die to-day," said Rayel, calmly. "He told me he would die to-day."

"He seems the same as usual," I said. "We cannot tell; he may live for months yet."

Rayel shook his head incredulously, and sat for a long time looking out of the window in silence.

"And I will go with you then?" he asked suddenly turning toward me.

"Yes," I answered.

It was the first time he had ever asked me a question, for he could read my mind like an open book, and to him all questioning was unnecessary.

While we were sitting there, thinking over our plans, my uncle summoned us by rapping with his cane. Rayel turned pale, and, with a whispered ejaculation, hurried out of the room and ran down the path to his father, followed closely by myself. My uncle was breathing heavily.

"Count it," said he, feebly extending his hand. Rayel counted his pulse-beats.

"Ninety-four, and growing quicker!" he exclaimed, turning toward me with a frightened look.

"It won't increase much," my uncle whispered, feebly, but with a cool and professional air. "It will go down soon, and then death will follow."

"Be calm, Rayel," he continued, almost sternly, as his son began weeping. "Be calm, I say! That music! do you hear it, child? Do you see what is passing now? Tell it. Let me hear you."

"I cannot hear it," said Rayel, looking earnestly into his father's face.

"Hallucination!" he whispered, groping about until his hand rested on the head of his son, who was kneeling beside him. "I seem to see millions of forms around me. I seem to hear them, but I cannot see you - nor hear you."

As if exhausted by the effort, his head fell back upon Rayel's shoulder, and he lay for a time, his eyes closed, struggling for breath. The dying man's faculties would no longer obey the whip of his mighty will. Indeed, they had done him their final service, for in a few moments he was dead. Tenderly and manfully, uttering no sound of grief, Rayel lifted the lifeless body of his father, and bore it into the house.

CHAPTER VII

In accordance with my uncle's wish, which he had made known to Rayel, we buried him the day following his death in the sunny courtyard where he had spent the last days of his life. The funeral arrangements were made as simple as possible, so as to exclude all except the functionaries whose presence was absolutely necessary. A rector of the Church of England read the service for the dead before the body was borne to its grave by the undertaker. When this brief ceremony was over, and the great gates were closed again upon our seclusion, Rayel said to me:

"I must talk more with you now, if you will let me. He said you would help me after he was gone."

It seemed idle to assure him, who already knew my heart, of the happiness it would give me to fulfill the pledge of friendship made to my uncle.

"Do you expect to see him again?" I asked.

After a moment of the most serious reflection, he said:

"Oh, yes, I shall see him again - when I die, then I shall see him. He has gone to the Great Father, who gives life, and who takes it away."

I found that Rayel, although entirely ignorant of the creeds and dogmas prevailing among men, was profoundly religious, and that his simple faith was built upon the deepest foundations. He evidently gave much thought to the relationship between man and his Creator after he felt the sting of bereavement, but it was a subject to which he never referred in our conversation, unless, perchance, it drifted in upon us.

The weeks following my uncle's death, during which I was busy with preparation for the new life that awaited us, Rayel spent in his studio working over some unfinished pictures. At my urgent request, he completed the head whose resemblance to Hester Chaffin had so startled and amazed me the night I saw it first, and he regarded it with fonder interest than he was wont to bestow upon the work of his brush. I believe that face was the closest presentment of a human soul I shall ever see until standing, as I hope to stand some time, in the presence of the redeemed, where "that which is imperfect shall be put away." I have said that the picture bore a strong resemblance to Hester Chaffin, but her face contained only a suggestion of that fine quality which was so strongly presented in my cousin's ideal.

My uncle's fortune, as described in his will, amounted to nearly $250,000. The greater part of it - everything, indeed, but the house and grounds - was in cash, represented by certificates of deposit accompanying the will, and bonds of the United States. There was a considerable bequest for me, whom he had named as executor of the will, which, however, I determined never to apply to my own use, except in case of Rayel's death. A handsome annuity was provided for his only surviving servant. The remainder was left to Rayel.

Having arranged for the maintenance of the old mute at an asylum not far from the city, our preparations to leave were soon complete. I was elated at the prospect of resuming my relations with the busy world outside that lonely habitation. My first step was to visit a lawyer for the purpose of ascertaining the legal formalities which I must observe as executor of the will. Rayel wished to go with me, and I gladly assented, for it seemed wise as an initiatory step in the new life that was awaiting him. He waved his hand to the mute, who stood looking at us through the big gates after we had passed out into the road, and then he walked on beside me in silence. The sun-shot haze of a beautiful autumn day hung over the face of nature, and his eyes wandered down the long stretches of landscape, and into the depths of the distant sky, rapt by the vision that was unfolding before him. The changing phases of the town he regarded with curious interest, which often expressed itself in childish exclamations of surprise as we made our way through the crowded streets.

He was constantly calling my attention to things which, though familiar and commonplace to me, were little less than wonderful to him.

"Look!" said he, suddenly taking hold of my arm. "There is a woman!"

He spoke in an eager, excited whisper, and shyly stepped behind me as she passed us.

"They won't hurt you," said I, subduing my desire to laugh at his remark.

Such unfamiliar exposure to the public eye soon began to grate upon his nerves. I did not wonder at it, for nearly every one we met took a second look at his commanding figure, and some stared at him rudely. Remembering my own emotions when I first stood in his presence, I was not at all surprised that others were moved in a like manner. His were a face and form that stood out like those of some heroic statue in the throng of common mortals.

The proving and recording of the will was left entirely in the hands of a reputable lawyer, who said that these formalities would not detain us longer than a week.

We had determined to spend the winter in New York before going to England. Since reaching America my time had been quite filled with work until my entrance upon the utter isolation of my uncle's home. It was my earnest desire to see something of the big metropolis on the western Atlantic. Moreover, Mr. Earl had advised me in his letters to give Rayel a chance to know more of life in his own country before bringing him to England.

When at last the faithful old mute had gone to his new home, and we had turned our backs upon the silent and deserted mansion, Rayel was moved to bitter tears. The thought of its loneliness, now that its master was dead and we were leaving it, perhaps forever, brought sad feelings to my heart. How calmly the old pines whispered together as we walked down the road that morning I shall not soon forget.

We reached the American metropolis early in October, three years after my first arrival there from England. I rented comfortable apartments on Fifth Avenue, near Madison Square. As soon as Rayel had recovered from the fatigue and excitement of the trip, we set about unpacking his pictures and getting them framed. Our lightest room was reserved for a studio, and the paintings were hung under Rayel's direction.

We were scarcely settled in our new home when we received an unexpected call from a newspaper reporter. He had learned from an art dealer that we had some remarkable old paintings, and humbly begged the privilege of looking at them. We made him welcome, of course, but I explained to him that the collection was wholly the work of my cousin, who was not yet old himself. In answer to his questions I assured him that the paintings would not be exhibited in the National Academy, and that my cousin's work had never appeared in any art exhibition whatever, at which he seemed greatly surprised. Rayel was still shy of strangers, and, as he was evidently a little annoyed at the presence of our visitor, I shielded him from the need of taking any part in our conversation.

The next morning an article appeared in one of the leading dailies, which subjected us to a glare of publicity not at all to our taste.

It went on to say that Signor Lanion, a young Spanish artist, had just arrived in New York and had taken apartments at No. Fifth Avenue. "Lanion" was the name which had appeared on our bill for picture-framing, the clerk who had waited on us having taken it down incorrectly. "Unfortunately," the article continued, "Signor Lanion does not speak English, and for that reason the reporter was unable to interview him."

The paper described Rayel's personal charms at much length, and claimed the credit of having discovered a genius who, although still a youth, had done work worthy of an acknowledged master.

We had deep respect for the influence of that newspaper before another week ended. Art managers, tailors, advertising agents, auctioneers and numerous men and women prompted by no motive but idle curiosity, besieged us until we bolted our doors in dismay against all comers. The mail, too, brought us missives of varying import from persons who had read the article, one of which was a polite letter from Francis Paddington, a Wall Street broker, whose name I had heard frequently during my American travels.

"It was not stated," said he, referring to the newspaper article, "whether or not any of Signor Lanion's paintings are for sale. If they are, I would be glad to look at them with a view to making some purchases for my art collection."

The letter suggested an idea worth considering. Rayel worked rapidly and had already painted more pictures than we could hang to advantage in any but the most liberal quarters. He was at a loss to understand just what was meant by selling the pictures, but he was willing to sell them if they were not to be destroyed - at least some of them. Accordingly I wrote Mr. Paddington, appointing an hour when we would be glad to see him or his representative at our rooms. The gentleman himself did us the honor to call. After looking at the paintings, he expressed his willingness to buy the entire collection. I told him, however, that we would not part with more than ten canvases, and he seemed glad to buy even that number at a price which was so far in excess of our expectations that I was loath to accept it. Our beloved "Woman" - that was the title we had given Rayel's strangely derived conception - was among the paintings included in the sale to Mr. Paddington. Rayel thought he could reproduce it, and for days after it was gone he made ineffectual efforts to paint another woman after the ideal of our hearts. But, alas! try as he would, that face never came back to his canvas. Many beautiful faces were conjured by his masterful touch, but they were other faces, and none of them satisfied us. The failure made Rayel unhappy, and tears came to his eyes when the "Woman" was referred to, as if he were mourning the loss of a dear friend.

Our patron had conceived a great liking for us, and we were soon invited to visit his house "and meet a few of his friends at dinner." It would give us an opportunity to see the "Woman" - perhaps to buy her back again - and we were strongly inclined to take advantage of it. Our patron's residence was one of the largest and most elegant on Fifth Avenue. It was a matter of common fame that his entertainments were the cause of more envy and heartburning in the fashionable sisterhood than any other events of the season. I had some doubt about the propriety of taking Rayel to such a place, unaccustomed as he was to the refinements and conventionalities of fashionable life. However, he had set his heart upon going - he was so eager to see his beloved picture - and I did not oppose his wish. In writing our acceptance of the invitation I corrected Mr. Paddington's error regarding our name, and explained the rechristening we had received in the public prints.

CHAPTER VIII

On the day of our appointment for dinner at Mr. Paddington's the newspapers were filled with accounts of a sensational bank robbery, which had occurred in Wall Street the night before. Between midnight and one o'clock in the morning, thieves had entered the Metropolitan Bank, overpowered the watchman, broken into the vaults and stolen half a million dollars in currency without leaving any clew behind them of the slightest value to the police. The subject interested Rayel intensely, and at our breakfast that morning we talked of little else.

"When they have found the thieves what will they do with them?" he asked.

"Send them to prison," I answered, "where thieves are kept apart from the rest of humanity."

"And yet these thieves were not in prison. They could not have robbed the bank if they had been in prison."

"True, but there are a good many thieves in the world who are not suspected. They look like honest men and are highly successful in concealing their dishonesty."

"I should think," he said thoughtfully, "that one would know a thief by his face."

"Remember," said I, "that all men are not like you. Most of them are easily deceived."

"Why, then, Kendric!" he exclaimed joyfully, "I can do some good with this power of mine."

This conversation may seem commonplace enough, but it stands in close relation to important events which will shortly claim our attention. The subject which it introduces was not soon abandoned. We talked about it on our way to the Paddingtons' that evening, where we were cordially received by our host, and introduced to a large company of ladies and gentlemen.

Rayel's wonderful skill with the brush had evidently been the subject of some discussion among Mr. Paddington's guests. It was referred to frequently, and somewhat to the embarrassment of my cousin, in the exchange of greetings that followed our introduction.

Greatly to the relief of my fears Rayel seemed quite at ease. He acknowledged the compliments paid him with gravity and self-possession, but with few words. All eyes were raised to his face, as he stood head and shoulders above a group of ladies and gentlemen who had gathered about him. Never had his presence seemed so magnetic and impressive since the first time I saw him in his father's house. Now, as then, a new inspiration was stirring his blood and charging every nerve with the wonderful magnetism of perfected manhood.

The last person presented to us was a young lady of unusual beauty, whom I noticed for some moments standing across the room in earnest conversation with our host. Presently he made his way toward us with the lady on his arm.

"My daughter, Mr. Lane, whom I shall ask you to escort to dinner," said he, addressing Rayel. After I had been introduced to the young lady she took Rayel's arm, and the company proceeded to the dining-hall. My seat at the table was almost directly opposite Rayel. His grave and dignified demeanor was made doubly conspicuous by the coquettish airs and ready tongue of the young lady who sat beside him. Under a steady fire of compliments and questions and artful glances I saw that he began to grow uneasy.

"That was a beautiful portrait you painted!" exclaimed Miss Paddington, looking sentimental.

"Thank you," said he; "my cousin also admires it, but I must own that it does not quite suit me."

"Perhaps you are an admirer of the lady it represents," said she, peering shyly into his eyes. "The Count de Montalle has fallen in love with her and has borrowed the portrait from my father."

"Ze picture - ah! monsieur, it is beautiful," said the Count, who sat near them. "But ze lady - she sat for me long ago and I had ze honor myself to paint her portrait."

He was a thin, wiry Frenchman, with small, black eyes, a forehead sloping to a bald crown, an aquiline nose and a pointed chin, adorned with an imperial. The face was almost mephistophelian in effect. He had painted her portrait! Was the man an impostor? I asked myself.

"The Count is an artist himself, you know," said Miss Paddington.

"Yes - an artist?" asked Rayel in a half-incredulous tone. Then he looked inquiringly at the gentleman referred to, as if doubtful of his own understanding of the words he had repeated.

"Yes," said the Count with emphasis. "For twenty years I have devote myself to ze art."

"To what art, sir?" asked Rayel, in a tone suggesting doubt.

I was now thoroughly frightened at the serious turn of the dialogue. Was this "Count" a pretender and one of the many bogus noblemen of whom I had read? Rayel was sounding him, that was quite evident. I saw now the mistake I had made in bringing my cousin to such a place.

"Quel impudence!" exclaimed the insulted nobleman, under his breath.

"Forgive me, sir," quickly answered Rayel, "I did not know it was wrong to ask you."

"I wish you would paint my portrait, Mr. Lane," said the young lady, who did not seem to appreciate the gravity of the situation.

"That would be easy enough," he answered.

"Would it? Ah, but I fear you would find me too plain a subject. I am not beautiful, you know, but if I wore my best clothes you might think I would do."

For some time Miss Paddington continued to spin out threads of small talk, while Rayel sat listening. The dinner was nearly over when the climax came which I had already begun to fear.

"It is strange," said Rayel thoughtfully. "You speak what is not true, Miss Paddington. You said that the Prince of Wales gave you the beautiful opal, but tell me - was it not your father who gave it you?"

He waited a moment for her answer.

"Oh, I understand now," he continued. "People do not always speak the truth - do they?"

The young lady turned red with embarrassment, while an unnatural smile played upon her lips.

"But - but what is the use of talking then?" he asked. No one seemed disposed to answer.

"It is strange," he continued, with childlike naivete, turning to the young lady sitting at his left, "you have been laughing as if you were very happy, but you have felt more like weeping. This must be a very sad world!" He ceased speaking as if some suspicion of the pain his words were causing had suddenly come to him.

The whole company turned its eyes upon the two. The young lady's face became suddenly pale and almost horror-stricken. Rayel's words were spoken in such a gentle and sympathetic manner that every one was mystified.

"Have you read about the great robbery that occurred last night?" asked Mr. Paddington, with the evident purpose of diverting attention from the young lady. "The vaults of the Metropolitan Bank on Wall Street were blown open with dynamite, and half a million dollars were stolen. No trace of the thieves has been discovered."

"Too bad!" exclaimed half a dozen of the guests seeking to enhance interest in the subject.

"Zey were very bold about it," said the Count, as he lighted a piece of sugar soaked in cognac and held it over his coffee.

Just at that moment a singular thing happened. The lights grew dim and suddenly went out, as if the gas had been turned off. The burning cognac cast a white flickering light upon the face of the man who had just spoken.

"You say there is no trace of the thieves," said Rayel. "That is strange, for one of them is in this room sitting at your table."

Only one face was visible, and all eyes were turned upon it, for now the effect of that pale light keeping it in view was indescribably weird. The eyes were suddenly turned in the direction of Rayel, and a devilish glare came in them for an instant, when the face suddenly seemed to shrink back into darkness. The ladies and some of their more gallant escorts rushed precipitately from the room. The servants hurried in with candles, but light was no sooner restored than the guests who still remained at table rose, as if by general consent, and left the dining-hall. Miss Paddington and Rayel were the last to leave the table. When they had passed out into the drawing-room her father came and took her arm, bowing coldly to my cousin. It was evident that our presence was no longer desired in the house of the Paddingtons. And no wonder!

"Let us go," I said, proceeding to the coat room. The Count met us on the way.

"You are a liar - a jackass!" he hissed into Rayel's ear.

Hastily drawing on our coats we stepped out into the chilly night air and walked leisurely down the deserted avenue. Neither of us spoke for some moments. Presently Rayel asked:

"What is a jackass?"

He stopped and took my hand as if expecting an answer of great moment.

"A man who always tells the truth in this world - he is a jackass," I replied.

I was a little irritated by the trying experiences we had been through. Perhaps that is why my answer savored so strongly of cynicism.

CHAPTER IX

Painful as had been our introduction to polite society, the reaction which followed it was scarcely less so. Next day we stayed indoors until evening, when we ventured out for a walk with fear and trembling lest the newspapers had already increased our fame and our mortification. The twilight of a cloudless autumn day was closing in upon the city, and the keen, bracing winds which sweep over the American metropolis from the sea brought the color to our faces. We walked down Broadway, now quite deserted, in silence, and as we were passing Wallack's Theatre Rayel stopped suddenly, and stood for a moment looking into the brightly lighted foyer. Stepping in, he beckoned me to follow. I immediately saw what had attracted his eye, for on an easel just inside the entrance was the portrait of our woman. On a placard below the picture was the name "Edna Bronson." Our surprise was mingled with sad regret at seeing it playing a false part to serve the ends of an unscrupulous manager.

"Perhaps she is here! suddenly exclaimed Rayel.

"That is very unlikely," I answered, "but we shall see."

I bought tickets for the evening's performance and we

hastened home, strangely elated, to dress for the play.

Our seats were in one of the lower proscenium boxes and quite clearly exposed to the gaze of the thousands who filled the theatre in winding rows, ascending and receding to the roof high above us. The garish decorations, the gay throng bedizened with jewels sparkling in the light and the hundreds of fair faces and bright eyes that were turned toward us presented a spectacle entirely new to Rayel. Shortly the curtain rose and the play began. Its first scene was a counterfeit of real stage life in an English theatre. An important performance is impending and at the last moment both the leading lady and her understudy are suddenly taken ill. The management is in a quandary. In the midst of its confusion the stage carpenter suggests that he has a daughter who can play the part. When this functionary came upon the scene my interest in the play began to wax stronger. Hester Chaffin's father had been a stage carpenter, and this turn in the scene startled me not a little after having found our picture in the foyer.

The carpenter's suggestion is at first treated with ridicule. He insists that she has learned the part from witnessing the rehearsals, and urges the managers to give her a trial. The performance must begin in four hours or be postponed. It is found that the costumes prepared for the part will fit the young lady. They consent to try her, the company is hastily summoned together for rehearsal, and the curtain falls on the first act. The audience waited impatiently for it to rise again and show what fortune might have in store for the carpenter's daughter, but of all that audience I was probably the most impatient.

"There is the Count," whispered Rayel, directing my attention to the opposite box. The diabolical little

Frenchman was there, sure enough, sitting next to the rail, and sweeping the audience with his opera-glasses.

Soon the curtain was rung up and the rehearsal began which was to test the powers of the venturesome young lady. Suddenly she appears at the rear of the stage dressed for her part in Elizabethan costume. She is greeted with loud applause, and she stands a moment, waiting for silence. The lights have been turned down and I cannot see her face distinctly. Before the last ripple of applause is quieted, she advances down the centre of the stage and begins to speak her lines. That voice! What is there in it that thrills me so strangely? When she ceases speaking she is standing almost within reach of my hand. Suddenly her eyes meet mine and I see Hester Chaffin standing there on the stage and looking into my face. She recognizes me, for she seems confused and proceeds with evident embarrassment.

I turned to Rayel - he, too, was deeply moved by this great surprise.

"Our woman has come to life," said he, in tremulous whispers. "I knew we would see her sometime."

How she had changed! She was little more than a child when I saw her last: now she was almost a woman, but not more beautiful than when I bade her good-by in the moonlight at her father's gate - long, long ago, it seemed to me now. Was the scene I had witnessed a passage in her own life since I had left Liverpool? At the close of the act an usher carried my card to her. Presently I was summoned to one of the corridors where a lady was waiting for me.

"Is this Kendric Lane?" she asked, extending her hand.

"It is," I responded.

"I have heard of you often. Miss Bronson is an old acquaintance of yours, whom you knew as Hester Chaffin. Would you like to see her?"

"I wish to see her to-night, if possible," said I.

"May I ask you, then, to go to this address and wait for us until the performance is over? Hand this card to the night clerk of the hotel and he will show you to our rooms."

Scribbling a few words upon the card, she gave it to me, and hurried behind the scenes.

Rayel and I immediately left the theatre and walked to our apartments. The play would soon be over and we had no time to lose. On the way home I noticed that he frequently turned about and peered through the darkness as if expecting some one to join us. He said nothing, however, and as I was so preoccupied by my own thoughts, I did not ask for whom he was looking.

"Shall I not go with you?" he asked, when we had reached home.

"You had better wait up for me; I shall not be gone long," I answered.

"I can walk back again when we get there, or perhaps I can wait for you in the hotel?" said he.

He was not yet accustomed to life in a great city, and it did not seem wise, either, to permit him to walk home alone, or to wait for me in the hotel among strangers. He did not seem quite content to stay, however, and there was a troubled expression on his face, which was new to it, and which I could not put out of my mind after I had left the house. The hotel to which I had been directed was on Union Square. It was not far from our apartments, and I intended to walk there, but I had not gone half a block before the street was lit up with a vivid flash of lightning, followed by deafening thunder, and the wind blew damp in my face. I hurried toward Third Avenue, intending to mount one of the horse cars going down-town, but suddenly a fierce gust of wind swept over me, sowing great drops of rain along the pavement. I looked about for a cab. The street was deserted and so dark that I could see nothing except the gloomy rows of brown stone that stood on either side. While I was looking backward another flash of lightning illumined the street. What man was that coming in the distance? Was it Rayel? No, that was scarcely possible. I had only caught a momentary glimpse of him in the quick flash. He was tall and erect like Rayel, and I thought the hat was his. But my imagination must have tricked me after all, for nothing showed clearly. I walked back a few steps and listened. I could hear no footsteps, but then he might have followed me, and I ought to be sure. So I called, "Rayel! Rayel!" twice, and waited for an answer, but could hear none. I had not time to go back to our rooms, as Hester was undoubtedly waiting for me now, and Rayel was certainly not the man I had seen, or he would have answered me. So I hurried along without giving any further thought to my fears. But where was Third Avenue? Its character was not then so sharply defined as in these days of elevated rail-roads - perhaps I had passed it. I had already walked a long distance, and I had not yet recognized that thoroughfare. I could hear footsteps behind me and I determined to wait a moment and inquire my way.

"I am going there - walk along with me," said the man whom I questioned. Just then we passed under a street lamp. I observed that he wore a large coat and muffler and that he was walking under an umbrella. Another man, also under an umbrella, fell in with us at the next corner. As we walked along in silence I heard some person coming at a run down the street quite a distance behind us. I was listening to this sound when I received a terrific blow on the back of the head. I fell forward, one side of my face striking heavily upon the pavement. Strangely enough, I seemed unable to make any outcry, but I had not lost consciousness, for, as I lay with my face resting on the wet stones, I could feel the rain drops falling on it. I could hear those quick footsteps coming nearer. Yes, I could hear Rayel's voice shouting in a loud and angry tone, but, try as I would, I could not utter a sound. As I listened, the two men clutched me with strong hands and dragged me through an open door, which quickly closed behind them. It was no sooner shut than Rayel threw himself against it with terrific force. I could hear the door groan and shake under the strain. Once - twice, I was struck with cruel force upon the head - then a loud roaring in my ears drowned everything.

I can remember well the first return of consciousness. It was like the slow breaking of dawn in the sky. I could hear voices singing:

Hark! hark! my soul! angelic voices swelling O'er earth's green fields and ocean's wave-beat shore.

I could just distinguish those words. Where was I? Strange thoughts began trooping through my mind. Then a great wave of emotion swept over me. I could hear a low moaning sound that came from my own throat. I could feel the hot tears rolling down my cheeks.

A gentle hand was brushing them away and some one was speaking to me. I was lying on a soft bed. A sweet-faced woman was bending over me, whom I had never seen before.

"Where am I?"

"In the hospital," she answered.

"The singing - who is singing?" I asked.

"It is the chapel choir," she answered; "the services are nearly over now. It is Sunday."

"Is Rayel here?"

"Your friend? yes, he has been with you every day."

"How long?"

"Almost a month."

I tried to ask other questions, but a drowsy feeling overcame me and I fell asleep.

When I awoke again Rayel was sitting beside me. As I opened my eyes he leaned over and kissed my hands.

"They thought you were dead once," he said; "but I knew you were not dead - I knew you were not dead." I lay for a moment trying to collect my thoughts. My head was in tight bandages and something was binding my chest.

"Where is Hester?" I asked. Rayel did not answer. He was not there, but somebody was holding one of my hands. It was a lady kneeling beside me, her face leaning forward upon the bed. Who could it be? I closed my eyes and listened to the rustling of withered leaves outside the window, and the low humming of insects in the autumn sun. These were prophetic sounds, and they opened the gates of thought and memory. A new life was coming now. What was it to be? Again I felt myself drifting into sleep. I tried to keep my eyes open and resist the drowsiness that overcame me, but in vain. When I awoke Rayel had returned.

"You have slept a long time," said he.

"When I fell asleep a lady was here."

"Yes, it was our 'Woman,'" he replied - "the lady you love. She has come every day to see you."

"Where is she now?"

"She had to go away, but she will soon come back again."

"Who brought me here?"

"I broke down the door - I found you there. You could not see me nor speak to me, but I knew you were not dead. The men were gone. I carried you out into the street. A policeman met me, and I told him what had happened. Then the ambulance came and we put you into it, and you were brought here. For a long time you lay like my father after he was dead. Your face was white - like snow. They had stabbed you in the side - they would have killed you if I had not broken the door."

"Who struck me?" I asked.

"I knew," he said, his eyes flashing, "I knew the devil was in their heads - that is why I wished to go with you. They followed us that night."

"Who?" I asked, eagerly.

"The Count de Montalle and another man."

My cousin's answer amazed me.

"Have you made known your suspicions?" I asked.

"No. I have been waiting to talk with you first."

"Do not speak of it yet to any one," I said. "Let us await developments."

I foresaw that Rayel would only get a reputation for insanity if pressed to the point of explaining his suspicions. It seemed quite likely, also, that any futile discussion of the subject would defeat justice.

That day brought me a letter from Hester, whom I had been looking for with much impatience since I had begun to feel more like myself. She would shortly have fulfilled all her professional engagements, and would then return at once to New York. "I wonder," she added, somewhat coquettishly, "if you will be glad to see me." On this point there was no doubt in my mind, and although my strength increased rapidly, the days passed with tedious slowness after that.

I was sitting by the window one morning, looking out upon the moving throng in the opposite street, when the door of my room was suddenly opened. I supposed that one of the physicians had come to see me, and I waited for him to speak.

"Kendric!"

It was Rayel who spoke my name, but somehow his voice did not seem quite natural, and I turned to greet him.

"This is our 'Woman,'" said he, advancing toward me with Hester upon his arm.

I rose feebly to my feet, confused by the sudden announcement, and took her extended hand. We looked into each other's eyes for a moment without speaking. My own were rapidly filling with tears, and I could see her but dimly.

"What a fine outlook you have!" she said, in a tremulous voice, turning suddenly to the window and looking out upon the trees now half stripped of their foliage by the autumn winds. We both stood staring out of the window in silence. For my part, I could not have spoken if I had known what to say. How she had changed! The blushing little miss who had awakened the pangs of first love in my youthful heart was a beautiful young woman, now full grown and arrayed in costly finery. Rayel was the first to speak.

"You must be glad to meet again - you have loved each other so long," said he.

Honest Rayel! He knew our hearts - their longings, their histories, and also the vanity and pride that dwelt in them. Why should there be any concealment between her and me?

"It has been a long time - a very long time to me, Hester,

for I have loved you ever since we first met."

She turned toward me, her eyes filled with tears, and I drew her to my heart and kissed her fondly.

"We have only known each other as children, Kendric," said she. "Your heart may change and mine may change - let us wait and see."

Then she left us, promising to come again next day.

CHAPTER X

Hester and her maid looked in upon me every morning after that, until I was able to leave the hospital. During these visits we told each other the eventful story of our lives since the night of our parting at her father's gate. Her first appearance on the stage had been, as I suspected, literally represented in the play. For years she had been permitted to accompany her father behind the scenes, and nights when the cast was short she had played small parts with great success. The glamour and excitement of stage life had proved distasteful to her. She assured me that it was her intention never to go back to it, and this strengthened my hope that she would some day consent to become my wife. Rayel had told her, during my illness, the strange story of his life. She knew nothing, however, of his wonderful powers, until I had related to her some of the experiences which had revealed them to me. He had said nothing to her, I learned, about our discovery of the picture.

"Who painted the remarkable portrait of you which we saw at the theatre?" I asked her one day.

"It was painted, I believe, by a French nobleman, who presented it to me here in New York. I suppose it looks a little as I did once, but it is certainly too flattering and much too maidenly for me now.

"The Frenchman is an impostor and worse," I said. "The portrait was painted by Rayel and sold to a broker of the name of Paddington, from whom the Frenchman borrowed or bought it."

Her amazement could scarcely be overestimated when I told her what occurred at Mr. Paddington's dinner-party.

"The Frenchman," she said, "has been paying me unwelcome attentions ever since the first night of my appearance in New York. He became so odious to me at length that I refused to accept any of his gifts, and, in spite of the protests of my managers, returned everything he had sent me, including the portrait."

I did not tell her that it was this same Frenchman to whom I was indebted for my wounds. Of that I must wait for more palpable evidence, though not for my own convincing. It seemed strange to me then that just at the moment this thought was passing through my mind she asked me whom I suspected of having committed the assault. It occurred to me after she had gone that possibly she had some cause to suspect the man who had been the subject of our conversation.

Rayel always came late in the day, when there was no chance of meeting other callers, and stayed with me until bedtime. As returning strength brought back to me that interest in life which prompts keen observation, I could see that a great change was coming over him. His face wore a melancholy look which indicated too clearly that his mind was suffering under some sad oppression. He was as gentle and considerate as ever, and as tireless in his efforts to increase my comfort, but he rarely spoke now, except in reply to my questions. He would sit by my side for hours, gazing out of the window with a vacant look in his eyes, until the light of day grew dim and the lamps were lighted. When supper was served to us I could never induce him to eat.

"What is the trouble, Rayel?" I asked, one evening. "You are not yourself lately."

Neither of us had spoken for a long time. He turned suddenly, as if startled by my words, his lips quivered, and stammering almost incoherently, he rose to his feet. Then he stood erect before me for a moment, looking sadly and thoughtfully into my eyes.

"Nothing, Kendric," he said presently, in a deep tone that trembled with emotion. "I think I have been working too hard and need exercise - that is all." Then he grasped my hand warmly and bade me good night.

I believe his answer to my question was the first lie that he had ever spoken.

CHAPTER XI

Next day I was discharged from the hospital, and Rayel and I were driven to our apartments. He had a number of surprises prepared for me. A large painting on his easel, awaiting some finishing touches, compelled my attention as soon as I entered the room. It represented a scene in our own lives, which had lasted but a second, but which could never be forgotten by either of us. He had seen me when I stood looking backward in that vivid flash of lightning - there could be no doubt of it now, for here was the scene transferred to canvas. The shaft of white light shaking and darting across the black sky like a gleaming sword; the man on the sidewalk looking backward with a startled glance; the big drops of rain falling sidelong in the wind - these were all reproduced on the canvas. His later pictures were characterized by a cynical tendency, which I observed with regret. It was evident that his sensitive mind had taken impressions from its brief contact with men, which were sadly affecting his thought.

He showed me numerous letters, many of which were from women who desired to visit his studio and see his work. Indeed, my cousin had apparently grown suddenly famous in the American metropolis. He was the victim rather than the victor of fame, however, and regarded the matter with very serious concern. The press of New York had been full of gossip concerning his "eccentricities" since the event which had put my life in danger. One of the society journals had printed a highly colored version of that little episode at the house of the Paddingtons, and had concluded its article by saying that the fair Miss Paddington had fallen madly in love with her father's strange guest.

That night, as we were sitting by the grate fire in our own rooms, Rayel, encouraged by our seclusion, began to emerge from the silence to which he had seemingly gone back for refuge in time of trouble.

"We shall soon be ready to start for England," I said.

"I do not wish to go to England, Kendric," said he. "For a long time I have thought over it. Let me go back to the old house and live by my father's grave, until the good Lord takes me to a better home. I would miss you, dear Kendric, and every day I would look for you to come, but I shall be happier there."

His words touched me deeply, and I was not prepared to answer him with perfect calmness, although I had lately suspected that his despondency would lead to this resolve.

"Why must we separate now, after we have become so dear to each other?" I asked. "Something has happened to change your purpose since I have been ill - tell me what it is."

"To speak frankly, Kendric, I must say that the world has sadly disappointed me. It is full of vanity and deceit and selfishness. Every day brings to me some hideous revelation which the mercy of heaven has hidden from others. I have seen the righteous forsaken of men, and the wicked receiving homage; I have seen the unjust triumphing over the just; I have seen some reveling in abundance while others were begging for bread. Everywhere I have found want and misery staring me in the face.

"Remembering what Christ said, I sold all I had and gave to the poor, and now there is nothing more I can do. My best pictures, my money and all my extra clothing have gone to feed the hungry and cover the naked. And even now, when I have nothing left to give, I find as much misery as before. Often, since I have been alone, I have had nothing to eat and no fire to keep me warm. Then I feared to tell you what I had done, and I bore it in silence, hoping that I might earn more money by painting. But I could not work. When Hester came back I told her all my troubles, and she gave me money, not only for my own use but for the use of others who needed it more than I. She and I have wandered about the city by day and by night, ministering to the sick and the friendless."

He ceased speaking, his head bent forward upon his hands. It was indeed a serious situation into which a too generous heart had betrayed him. Nearly all his fortune had descended to him in cash on deposit, and payable either to my order or to his. He had therefore saved nothing for himself that had been available for the satisfaction of his good impulses. Instead of displeasing me, however, as he feared, his action only increased my love for him, if that were possible.

"Do not let these things trouble you, Rayel," I said. "We shall find no difficulty, I think, in earning money enough for our needs. I cannot see you shut yourself away from the world: you have yet an important work to do among men. You are now morbidly sensitive to the misery that surrounds us, but you will feel it less keenly as it grows more familiar."

"You do not understand me, Kendric," said he, starting from his chair, and pacing restlessly up and down the room. "I cannot deceive you any longer. In begging you to leave me, it is your own happiness I am thinking of. Please go as soon as possible," he pleaded, laying his hand gently upon my shoulder. "Take her with you, and let me stay."

My heart seemed suddenly to have stopped beating.

"My God, Rayel!" I exclaimed. "Are we both in love with the same woman?"

"No, Kendric, no," he said quickly, taking my hand. "I do not mean that. I would not permit myself to love her, knowing that you love her also."

"What, then, do you mean?" I asked.

"That there is danger," he answered huskily, sinking into a chair. "I am a fool not to have thought of it long ago!"

His words seemed to sting me, and for a moment I could not speak.

"You know what is in her heart, Rayel," I said presently. "Tell me, is it false, or is she, as I have thought, a pure and noble woman?"

"She is pure and worthy of your love," he answered.

"Her life has been much exposed to temptation, but her character has been greater than any temptation. When she began to go with me among the poor I did not know what love was. I had never felt the power of it, nor did I think of the danger to all of us. When at last it came upon me, and I saw what it meant, I resolved not to see Hester again until God had given me strength to subdue that passion. For days my heart was near breaking. When you asked me to tell you what made me sad, I had not the courage to do it. Then I told you a lie. I did the very thing which I have so much condemned in others. This trouble has taught me to comprehend and to pity the frailty of men. I look forward with fear and dread for my own sake.. I shall be safe in my father's house. I must go back, but, before I go, forgive me. Tell me that you do not despise me."

As he ceased speaking he laid his hand upon my shoulder and peered into my face with a frightened and appealing look.

"Despise you!" I repeated. "No. You are dearer to me now than ever. What you have told me will bring us closer to each other, if we consider it wisely. As yet there is no pledge between Hester and myself, save the assurance given by unuttered thoughts. Her heart is free. I have no right to claim it. If she loves you I shall wish you both much joy."

"That will not be necessary, Kendric. I had rather die than know that I had come between you. I cannot even risk the danger of it. I must leave you to-morrow."

"Under no circumstances will I consent to that. My promise to your father and my duty to you forbid it. To go back now would be cowardly and unworthy of you.

With my help and guidance you can do great things. We must face the world with stout hearts. As to this trouble, let us concern ourselves about it as little as possible. I believe that whatever may be best for all will happen if we but wait with patience."

Rayel made no answer, and for some moments we both sat looking at the glowing embers in silence.

"I shall obey your wish," he said presently; "I cannot do otherwise. I am like a child, and must look to you for instruction in all things. Perhaps there will come a time when I can repay you."

"It will be a pleasure for me to help you as I would a brother, and you will owe me no gratitude for it," I said.

We sat discussing our plans for the future until near midnight. When we went to bed at last, Rayel looked happier than I had seen him before since my recovery at the hospital.

When I awoke it was near midday. I went to call Rayel and found that he was gone.

CHAPTER XII

After waiting for him nearly an hour I went to a neighboring restaurant for breakfast. On returning I found that he had not yet come back. Alarmed at his continued absence I went at once to Hester's apartments, scarcely expecting, however, to find him there, but confident that she would be able to tell me where he was likely to go.

"No doubt he has gone on some good errand," she said. "Has he not told you of his charitable enterprises?"

"He told me last night how they had reduced his fortune."

"Poor fellow!" she continued. "In his zeal for others he quite forgot his own needs. I would have told you about it, but that he implored me to spare you any knowledge of his condition. I think we shall be able to find him. Let us go and try."

Hester and I set out at once, walking rapidly against a biting east wind toward the river. On reaching Second Avenue we took a car and rode down among the big tenements towering into the sky on all sides in the lower part of the city. Alighting in the midst of these human hives, we made our way through a wretched crowd, shivering in the livery of destitution, down a long and narrow alley. Entering one of the doorways we climbed a steep flight of stairs, above which was a squalid throng pressing about an open door on the landing. The women held children in their arms, and many of them were crying bitterly. The men stood in silence peering curiously over the heads of the further throng into the crowded chamber. Some of them greeted Hester with great respect, and moved aside that we might have room to enter. As we neared the door I could hear a babel of strange tongues and the voices of women calling down the blessings of Heaven upon some one in their midst. It was Rayel. He stood in a corner of the room holding two little children in his arms, and the crowd was pressing forward as if eager to speak with him. He was talking in a low voice to those nearest him, but I was unable to catch his words. There were men and women of many nationalities in the throng. 1 saw Italians, Celts, Poles, Germans and even men whose swarthy faces and peculiar garb betokened Syrian origin. When we pressed nearer to Rayel I saw some, as they came within reach, extend their hands and touch him fondly, uttering exclamations as they did so, often in a tongue that was strange to me. These simple-minded people seemed to regard him as a supernatural being whom it was good to talk with, and whose touch it was a blessing to feel. A look of love and gentleness and sympathy irradiated his face and invited their confidence. These were evidently the poor whom he had befriended, and he was now taking leave of them, probably forever. It was a scene the like of which few can ever hope to witness. After all, I thought, what manner of riches can be compared to the satisfaction which Rayel feels at this moment? I was quite ready then to applaud his unselfish generosity, for in that gloomy and unclean place I first saw the full radiance of God's truth that it is infinitely more blessed to give than to receive. We stood for a long time looking upon this memorable meeting of Cadmus and Caliban. When at length he caught sight of us, Rayel came where we stood, and said he was ready to go home. Perceiving that we were about to go, the crowd hurried from the building into the narrow alley leading out upon the street. Some shouted endearing farewells as we passed them, and many of their hardened faces were wet with tears. The sun was just going down and the shadows were deepening between the high walls looming above us as we started homeward. Hester insisted that we must dine with her and decide upon the day of our departure. Rayel and I went directly home for a bath and a change of clothing, after which we proceeded at once to Hester's apartments. Evidently somewhat fatigued by the day's experience, Rayel had little to say while we were eating dinner. It was arranged that we would start for England by the first steamer on which we could secure a comfortable passage. We had no sooner finished our coffee than a servant announced Mr. Benjamin Murmurtot, who wished to see Miss Bronson.

"A reporter!" exclaimed Hester. "There's no dodging them in America. Shall I ask him in for a moment?"

We said yes, of course, and Mr. Murmurtot presently fluttered into the room. He was a natty little man, with a large nose, a bald head and a decidedly English accent.

"Delighted to see you, Miss Bronson," said he, "delighted, I'm sure. Thought I'd call and pay my respects before you leave the city."

He greeted us all with like effusiveness and sat down facing Hester.

"It's very kind of you," said she; "but pray how did you know I was to leave the city?"

"Why, I'm sure, Miss Bronson, everybody knows you are going home to be married?"

"It is true that I am going home soon," said she, "but I must decline to discuss my object in doing so."

"Pray pardon me; I'm a journalist, you know," said Mr. Murmurtot, "and I earn my living by impertinence. Have I not seen you before, sir?" he continued, facing Rayel. "I think you were at the theatre one evening some time ago - sat in the lower box at the right of the stage - I remember it well, sir."

"I remember the occasion," said my cousin, with his accustomed gravity.

"I read about that occurrence at Mr. Paddington's dinner-party, sir," continued Mr. Murmurtot. "It was decidedly clever in you, sir - deucedly clever! Everybody is talking about it, now that the Count has been arrested."

"Arrested!" I exclaimed; "has he been arrested?"

"Yes, this morning, for the robbery, you know. They say that the police have secured evidence that will convict him sure, but it seems they are not yet ready to make it public; reporters can't get the Inspector to say a word about it, you know - not a word."

There were exclamations of surprise and gratification from all present, save Rayel, who remained silent, while a faint smile stole over his face.

"I knew they would find him out," said he.

"I hear that you are a mind-reader, sir," said Mr. Murmurtot, again addressing my cousin.

"And you are a detective, I believe, and not a reporter," said Rayel. "It is good that we understand each other."

Mr. Murmurtot started with surprise at the remark.

"I do not know how fully you may be acquainted with my secret," said he, "but permit me to assure you that I am here on a friendly mission.

"I have no doubt of that," said my cousin.

"Let me proceed directly to the object of my visit, then, which is to learn how soon you expect to return to England."

"By Saturday, if possible," I replied.

"That is good," said he, turning toward me. "The sooner the better. In the meantime it will be my duty to keep a sharp eye upon you; I have been near you all day. You need not feel any alarm - only do not be surprised if you meet me often. I am responsible for your safety, that is all."

"For whom are you acting?" I asked.

"My dear sir," said he, rising to go, "men in my line of business must not talk too much. Good night."

After he had gone we asked Rayel to tell us more about this mysterious visitor, but he was unable to do so.

When we started away Hester put on her wraps and walked with us to the cab. As we alighted at our own door I saw a man standing by the street lamp on the corner, some distance away, whom I recognized as Mr. Murmurtot. I found a letter from Mr. Earl awaiting me at home, in which he urged us to hasten back to England as soon as possible after my recovery.

"You and Rayel," he said, "will, I trust, make your home at my house."

Next day we began our preparations for the voyage.

CHAPTER XIII

It was on a bleak and windy night in December that we were driven through a pelting rain to one of the docks on the North River, which our steamer was to leave at high tide in the early morning. When we alighted Mr. Murmurtot stood shivering in a greatcoat and muffler close by the passengers' entrance.

"This is a good place for a warm greeting," said he, taking Hester's hand. "I've stood here so long that my teeth are chattering from the cold."

"Won't you come aboard with us?" I asked.

"Not yet," he replied; "but I expect to sail with you in the morning."

"'Sa rough night, sir," said the porter who carried our luggage, "but we'll find it a bit rougher outside, I'm feered, afore anither night."

Fatigued by a long day of arduous work, we went at once to our staterooms. I was soon asleep after getting into my berth, but was awakened by the tramp of feet on the upper decks and the shouting of the crew long before the ship left her moorings. They reminded me of the first night I had ever spent on an ocean steamer - the night I left Liverpool on that journey fraught with danger I had not then dreamed of. I had grown old very fast under the influences that had come into my life since then. Indeed, I was now a man, whereas I had been only a boy when I left England. But Rayel was with me now, and that repaid me for all I had suffered. What would he have done in that lonely mansion after his father's death? For hours my mind was occupied with these reflections, and at length I determined to dress myself and go on deck. Rayel awoke while I was dressing and decided to go with me.

We found the decks thronged with people, and the ship's crew were bustling about, getting ready to sail. We stood near the gangway, facing the dock. A man was pacing back and forth in the opening whose figure seemed familiar to me. Presently he came aboard, and as he passed near us I saw it was the omnipresent Mr. Murmurtot.

"I wonder if he is afraid somebody will steal the ship?" I remarked.

"No, he is looking for some person," said Rayel, divining my thoughts.

"All ashore! Stand away, there!" shouted one of the ship's officers.

The passengers fell back, the gangway was pulled aboard, the great hawsers were loosened, and the ship moved slowly away from the dock. We stood for a long time watching the river craft and the receding lights of the city. The ship was well beyond the Atlantic Highlands when we went to our stateroom and to bed again. We slept until late in the morning, and arose barely in time for a late breakfast with Hester. Rayel seemed cheerful enough and took more than ordinary interest in his surroundings. When we had risen from the table he led me aside and directed my attention to a short, stout man with a bristly growth of close-cropped black hair, a low forehead and shaggy eyebrows, who was leaning lazily against the railing of the stairway.

"Let us avoid him," he whispered. "I do not like his looks."

What can this mean? I asked myself, as we all proceeded to the deck. Perhaps he was the man the detective was looking for.

It was a beautiful sunlit afternoon, and the vessel rode steadily in a sea that was growing quiet under the dying impulse that the winds had left behind them. We drew our chairs together on the deck near the stern of the vessel, and had settled down for a quiet chat among ourselves when we were unexpectedly joined by Mr. Murmurtot.

"Delighted, I'm sure!" he exclaimed, with the same inimitable drawl I had noted on the occasion of our first meeting. I soon observed that the artful little gentleman was master of an elaborate system of exclamations by which he encouraged one to talk freely without saying anything himself.

In response to my assertion that we had been exceedingly busy getting ready for the trip he said simply: "Indeed!"

It was a very unusual burst of confidence in which he was moved to express his views with any greater freedom.

When the remark which preceded it was evidently expected to meet with Mr. Murmurtot's concurrence, then he would say, "Yes, indeed!"

If the remark were one to which this response would be inappropriate he often went to the extent of observing, "I dare say!" seemingly ventured after careful consideration of the chances for and against the proposition which provoked it.

"My dear sir, I do not agree with you," he would always say when he felt compelled to differ with me. If the difference in our views chanced to be extremely radical, he would throw particular emphasis upon the word "dear," as a sort of recompense for his opposition. These forms of speech, with occasional and slight variations, were always employed by Mr. Murmurtot as a medium of thought and sentiment.

In the midst of our conversation I noticed the man whom Rayel had pointed out to me when we arose from the breakfast-table. He was standing against the rail, not twenty feet from where we sat, and as I looked at him he turned away and walked leisurely down the deck. In a moment Rayel was on his feet, and, excusing himself, he proceeded in the same direction. An hour later, as he had not returned, I left Hester with Mr. Murmurtot and went forward in quest of him. He was in the reading-room, apparently interested in a newspaper. As he did not observe me, I sat down behind his chair without disturbing him. To my surprise I saw that he was not reading the paper, but that his eyes were furtively watching the mysterious stranger he had followed, who sat on the other side of the room listlessly puffing at a cigarette. I was seated scarcely a moment when Rayel seemed to be aware of my presence. Looking from face to face until he had discovered me he arose and came to my side.

"I was trying to read a newspaper," said he, leading the way to the door, "but reading is still hard work for me."

"I saw that you did not seem to be looking at the paper," said I, as we proceeded to the deck. He made no reply, but stopped and looked out across the waste of waters at the horizon.

"Do you know that man?" I asked.

For a moment I stood waiting for his answer. Apparently he had not heard my question, and I repeated it in a somewhat louder tone.

He turned suddenly with an impatient exclamation. There was a flash of anger in his eyes as he faced me. I had never seen him in such a mood before.

"Forgive me," said he. "I am only angry with myself. Come, Hester will be looking for us."

I did not venture again to refer to our bristly fellow-passenger in Rayel's presence. Never inclined to talk much, even with me, he was becoming more silent than ever as the voyage continued. Day by day his interest in that strange man seemed to increase. He spent as little time as possible in my company. When not with me he was hounding him about the ship, keeping him in sight from some favorable point of observation. What was the meaning of it? The question forced itself upon my mind persistently by day and night, and begat in me a gloomy reticence which Hester was quick to observe. Every day I expected some revelation from Rayel, but he said nothing about the man in whom he had taken such extraordinary interest.

We had been over a week at sea, and I was sitting alone one afternoon, when Mr. Murmurtot came along and asked if he might introduce an acquaintance of his whom I ought to know. Then he went to find the gentleman, saying that he would return in a few moments. He had no sooner left me than my mind reverted to the man who had been the bugbear of my thoughts since we left New York. Presently Mr. Murmurtot touched my arm. Looking up suddenly, I saw standing before me the very man of whom I had been thinking.

"Mr. Lane, let me introduce you to Mr. Fenlon," said the detective. I shook the hand that was extended to me mechanically, and made some incoherent response - I do not remember what. I had been taken by surprise. My voice was unnatural and my strength seemed to have left me suddenly.

"Are you not well, sir?" he asked.

"No, sir, he is not well yet."

It was the voice of Rayel that answered for me. He was standing by my side, his lips tightly drawn, and his eyes fixed upon the man Fenlon. There was a terrible look on his face as he stood there towering above us. The man turned pale and moved quickly backward two or three steps, staring at my cousin as if in fear of receiving a death-blow. For an instant, only, he stood like some fierce animal at bay, then turned and walked hurriedly down the deck. The situation was made all the more impressive by the interval of silence that followed Rayel's words.

"Forgive me," said Mr. Murmurtot, taking my hand, "if this meeting was unpleasant. It was necessary." Then he bowed politely and walked away. The sun was just going down as Rayel and I entered the cabin, where Hester was waiting for us.

"The captain thinks we will reach Southampton before five in the morning," said she.

I was glad to learn that our voyage was so near its end.

CHAPTER XIV

After dinner Rayel and I went at once to our stateroom.

"I am out of patience with myself," said he, as soon as we were seated. "My mind is failing me just when I need it most. I have grown dull and stupid. For more than a week I have been trying to find out that man's secret. I knew that he had a secret, and that it concerned us. Not until to-night was I certain that I had found it out. Once I could see the truth clearly. No matter how deeply it was buried under lies - I could see it. But now there is something like a mist before my eyes, and I am sure of nothing. Perhaps it is because I am now a liar myself, as bad as any of them. God have mercy on me!" said he, rising, and speaking with much animation. "I know now what is blinding my soul. When a man lies he loses some degree of his power to distinguish between truth and falsehood."

He stood looking into my face impatiently, as if waiting to hear what I would say to his remark.

"That would be the natural result, I have no doubt," said I; "but are you not trying to convict yourself of too much wickedness and stupidity?"

I had never considered the misfortune of knowing too much - of being able to detect every difference between word and thought, between appearance and reality. That was the power which Rayel possessed, and it increased his moral responsibility by as much as it transcended the power common to others. Here, indeed, was a man ripe for the fate of a martyr.

"Won't you tell me Fenlon's secret, if you have found it out?" I asked. "I've been thinking about it night and day since we first saw him."

"Be wise! Don't try to learn too fast, Kendric" said he. "You shall know it soon, I am sure of that - indeed, I promise that you shall."

"I am quite willing to wait on the future for everything if you think it is best," I said.

We sat for a long time, making plans for our future life in England. It was near midnight when we retired to our berths, but we were up early in the morning, eager to catch the first sight of land. On reaching the deck we were overjoyed to see the distant spires of Southampton glowing in the morning sun.

CHAPTER XV

Mr. and Mrs. Earl met us at the station of the Southwestern Railway in London, and we were driven at once to their home. Hester came to breakfast with us, but Mrs. Earl would not let her go to Liverpool that day, ship-worn and fatigued as we all felt after the voyage.

"You resemble your father, sir, when he was of your age," said Mr. Earl, addressing my cousin, as we were eating. "But you are larger, much larger, than he was."

"You were my father's friend when he was a young man, I believe?" said Rayel.

"Yes, he and his brother were my best friends in those days. I tried to induce him to study law, but he was more inclined to medicine."

Rayel had found a man quite after his liking and the two were on the best of terms at once. Indeed, he seemed to talk with my benefactor as freely as he ever talked with me. I found Mrs. Earl very much as I had imagined my mother to have been - a full-faced, ruddy-cheeked woman; with a sweet voice and gentle manners. She greeted me as if I were her own son returned from a long journey, and when we sat down to talk after breakfast, I felt the joy and peace of one who has found a home after much wandering.

I spent the afternoon with Mr. Earl in his library, and he listened with deep interest to the complete story of my life since the night we parted in Liverpool.

He had many questions to ask me touching the attempt upon my life, and my replies were jotted down in his memorandum-book. After I had told him all that I was able to tell he sat for some moments thoughtfully turning the pages of the book, stopping now and then to read some of the memoranda.

"It looks pretty bad for them, doesn't it?" said he calmly, looking up at me over his spectacles. "But we'll bring this matter to a climax very soon," he continued. "We haven't seen the last act of the play yet. You need not have any further fear for your safety - I will look after that. You may feel quite free to go and come as you please in this part of the city. Above all things we must avoid letting them know that we suspect anything; it might defeat me in getting hold of the last bit of evidence that is necessary to complete our case."

I nodded, and waited for him to proceed.

"Let us go carefully until we're sure of our ground," he continued. "Your stepmother knows you are in London, of course. You must go and see her. Take your cousin with you, and - well, you will know how to treat them. After all, you must bear in mind that in the eye of the law every man is innocent until he is proven guilty. Adopt that view of the case yourself. You needn't fear anything from Cobb or his wife. Only be reasonably prudent."

"I've no fear that they will try to do us any harm," said I; "and I would greatly enjoy visiting the old house. Perhaps we could go to-morrow."

"The day after. You'd better go down to Liverpool to-morrow with the young lady, and return by the night train."

That day saw the beginning of a deep and lasting friendship between Hester and Mrs. Earl. When we left next morning to go to Hester's home in Liverpool, she promised to return soon for a long visit. By ten o'clock we were well out of smoky London, on the way that I had already traversed once before, with a cheerful heart most creditable to me under the circumstances. Mrs. Chaffin was waiting for us at the gate when we alighted in front of the old wood-colored cottage - that haven of weary legs in days gone by. Phil (who had lengthened noticeably in the service of Valentine, King & Co.) was there, too, and all the rest of the Chaffin household in Sunday clothes. Mrs. Chaffin was quite beside herself with joy.

"Dear-a me!" said the good lady, after the salutations were over. "Dear-a sakes! How you've growed! I didn't think you'd ever live to get s' big. I thought as 'ow som' 'arm 'd come to ye when ye went away, an' Hester -"

"Mamma!" exclaimed Hester, with a reproving glance. "Don't tell him."

"I'm that fidgety I don't know what I'm sayin'. The Lord bless us, but ye must be hungry!" said the good woman, as she spread the table for dinner. She had guessed rightly, and Hester bustled about, helping her mother get the dishes on the table, with a critical eye to all the arrangements. Rayel was much amused by the children, the youngest of whom had climbed upon his knee and was taking liberties with his cravat. He was wholly unaccustomed to the pranks of children, and we frequently rallied to his defence. He seemed to enjoy them, however, and was soon involved in a spree at which both Hester and I laughed heartily.

"This herring ain't extra good, sir, but I 'ope it won't go ag'in' ye," said Mrs. Chaffin to Rayel, as we sat down to the table.

He seemed in doubt for a moment as to what it would be proper to say in reply to this well-intended remark.

"I have never eaten a herring, madam," said he, gravely, "but I have no doubt it will be good."

"I 'ope so, sir - indeed, I 'ope so; but I dare presume to say that it will taste bad enough to the likes of you."

Mrs. Chaffin (good soul) had evidently concluded that my cousin was a man entitled to extra politeness. Hester had adroitly side-tracked the herring question and started another train of speculation, when her mother's misgivings were again excited respecting the tea, which Rayel had just tasted.

"Murky, sir?" she asked, with a glance of alarm. "I 'ope it don't taste murky."

Mrs. Chaffin's solicitude respecting the tea and the herring reminded me of the first time I had stretched my tired legs under that hospitable board at Phil's invitation; of those big, wondering eyes that stared at me across the table; of the songs and stories which beguiled the evening hours.

The candles were lit before dinner was over, and when we rose from the table it was to gather about the warm fire and exchange memories, while Rayel listened with deep interest. Phil had been promoted from a pair of legs to a pair of hands, and was now third bookkeeper for the firm. Our carriage came for us at nine o'clock. Hester had decided to stay a day or two with her mother, but it was necessary for Rayel and me to return to London that night, as we were to make an important call the next day.

CHAPTER XVI

Late in the afternoon of the day following our visit to Liverpool we ascended the big stone steps of my old home and pulled the bell. After all, I found that my nerves were not quite steady while we were waiting for the door to open. We had come intending to spend the night there, and my benefactor had given me certain precautions not calculated to make me feel entirely at home. Was there some deeper plan underlying his suggestion as to this visit than he had chosen to explain? I had not long to consider that point, however, for suddenly the door opened and a servant in imposing livery confronted us. I handed him my card and we were shown into the reception room at once. Presently he conducted us to my stepmother, who greeted me with a great show of cordiality and some tears. She had grown old fast since I left home, but she had artfully disguised the evidences of age upon her face and neck. Why had I stayed away so long? What had she done to deserve such shameful neglect? These and other questions taxed my wits for an answer that would neither outrage my own conscience nor offend her. Mr. Cobb, who had just returned from his office, suddenly entered the room. His face assumed an ashen pallor, and he stared at me quite dumfounded for a moment, when I arose and stood before him.

"It is Kendric. Don't you recognize him?" said my stepmother.

"So it is!" he exclaimed. "But he's grown quite out of my recollection." The man had recovered his self-possession in a moment, and treated me, it must be said to his credit, with marked coolness. I was likely to get on with him very well, I thought, but the fawning attitude of his wife quite unhorsed me. If I am to see the devil I'd rather he'd frown than smile. Cobb had very little to say to us, and left the room at the first opportunity. In doing so he had shown scant consideration for his wife, however, as it left a burden upon her shoulders that must have taxed her strength. But she was not unequal to it. Her smile broadened after he had gone, and there was a tone of deeper sincerity in her expressions of regard. We had been to dinner, and if she would kindly send a little cold lunch to our room at bedtime that would be quite sufficient. During her absence for dinner the reaction came. When my stepmother returned she seemed to have suddenly grown older, and she looked at us through haggard and sunken eyes. Surely this was a terrible punishment she was undergoing, and I pitied her. Mr. Cobb had an important engagement to keep, she said, and hoped we would excuse him. Slowly the evening wore away and at ten o'clock we were shown to our room, greatly fatigued by this trying experience. It was a room fronting the street on the third floor, which I had occupied before I left home. The walls had been painted white since then, with a frieze of gold along the ceiling. My father used to sleep in the room directly under it. Rayel had been silent and absent-minded all the evening, rarely speaking except in reply to some question.

"I feel sad for some cause I do not understand," said he,

preparing to retire. "I shall be glad when to-morrow comes."

"We will go back in the morning," I said. "You don't feel at home here, do you?"

He did not seem to hear me, but tried the door, which I had already bolted, and then got into bed, yawning and shivering, for the room was cold. I turned down the light, and, opening the shutters, looked out upon the street, now deserted save by a solitary man who had just passed the house and whose slow footsteps were gradually growing less distinct. I crouched there, listening for some moments to that fading sound, when it began to grow louder again. The man had turned about and was coming back. As he passed under the lamp on the opposite corner I thought I recognized the slim figure of Mr. Murmurtot. Suddenly I was startled by a noise in the room adjoining ours, and sprang to my feet in a tremor. Plague take my imagination! It was somebody going to bed. I sat down again and for a long time looked out at the man walking back and forth in front of the house. I was rapidly getting into a condition of mind unfavorable to rest and, closing the shutters, I went to bed at once. For hours I lay tossing restlessly from one side to the other, and finally fell into a deep sleep. I must have slept a long time when I suddenly awoke, laboring with nightmare. I had heard no sound, I had felt no touch, but all at once my eyes were open and I knew that I was awake. The lamp was burning dimly on the table beside my bed. How my heart was beating! And my arm - how it trembled when I tried to raise up on my elbow and look about the room!

"Who's there?" I whispered. Was it Rayel standing near the bed, his body swaying backward and forward, or was

IRVING BACHELLER

I yet asleep? Everything looked dim and weird. I seemed to be in some silent ghostland between sleeping and waking. I rubbed my eyes and peered about the half-darkened room. It was Rayel, and, as I gazed at him, his eyes seemed to shine like balls of fire. I called to him, but he made no answer. What had happened since I went to sleep? Alarmed, I threw the covers aside and leaped out of bed. As I did so he stepped up close to the opposite wall, and, as his hand moved, I could hear the grating of a crayon on its surface. In tremulous haste I turned up the wick of the lamp and tiptoed toward him, holding it in my hand. He was stepping backward and excitedly pointing at the wall. He had been drawing a picture on its white surface - the form of a woman holding something in her hand. I stepped nearer, still carrying the lamp. A sharp interjection broke from my lips. The woman pictured there was my stepmother, and it was a knife that she held! A man was lying at her feet. Again Rayel stepped forward, and again I heard the crayon grating on the wall. Then he stood aside. Great God! There were drops of blood dripping from the knife now. Rayel sank down upon the floor and covered his eyes with his hands. I stood there, dumb with fear and horror, looking first upon him and then upon the picture.

The silence of the night was unbroken save by those slow footsteps in the street to which I had listened before retiring. But suddenly I heard a low wailing cry in the room adjoining ours. It so startled me that I came near dropping the lamp. Strange and weird it sounded, gradually growing shriller and more terrible to hear! It was the voice of my stepmother. Was she dreaming? And had Rayel seen the vision that affrighted her? Was that dagger pricking her brain? In a moment the swelling cry broke into a sharp scream, such as might come from one exposed to sudden peril, and ceased. Then the sound of a bell rang sharply through the house, followed by loud knocking at the door and a man's shout.

"Open the door, I command you!" he said.

He must have heard that piercing cry. Rayel still lay motionless upon the floor. Was he asleep? Why did he not rise? I began to feel numb. I seemed to have lost the power of motion. I could hear some one rapping at our door, but I could not move.

"Kendric! Kendric! Kendric!" Was it my stepmother who was calling me? What a piteous, pleading tone! "Let me speak to you, Kendric! For God's sake, let me tell you!" I was reeling: my strength had all left me. Crash! went the lamp at my feet. There was a great flash of light, which dazzled my eyes, and I fell heavily upon the floor.

I was in the open air when thought and feeling came back to me. My hands and face were paining me as if they had been terribly burned. There were a number of men standing over a motionless figure that lay beside me.

"The poor lad!" said one of the men "he's nearly roasted. See here how the clothes have been burned away from his neck! Can't ye stop the blood? The mon'll die afore the amb'lance comes ef we don't stop the blood. A brave mon he is, too. D'ye see 'im coming down the stairs with th' other one on his back?"

Of whom were they talking? I struggled to my feet - I could feel no pain now - and bent over that still form which had been lying beside me. Oh! it was the heaven-blessed face of Rayel, now bleeding and scarred and ghastly. I raised his head. The hair fell away where my hand touched it, and a groan escaped his lips. I could not speak nor weep nor utter any sound. A strange calmness came over my spirit and I sat there motionless, bending over him I loved so well, while the crowd of men looked on in silence. "After His own image made He man;" these words came to my mind as I looked into that dear face. Then I prayed in silence - for him. Thank God! his eyes were open now and his lips were moving. I bent lower until I could feel his breath upon my cheek.

"Is it you, Kendric?" he whispered. "Did I save you from the fire? I cannot see you, but I know you are here."

I heard his words distinctly, but I could not answer. The power of speech seemed to have left me.

"The fire awoke me," he continued, moaning. "We were lying on the floor. I called to you, but you did not answer. Thank God! you are safe now."

Returning consciousness brought with it an increasing sense of his pain, and he began to struggle and groan in dreadful agony. Suddenly, extending one of his blackened hands until it touched my face, he shouted in a loud voice:

"Kendric! Kendric! help - help me!"

Then some men laid hold of me and lifted me up. I clung to Rayel with all my strength, but could not resist them, and as I was borne away I knew that Rayel and I had parted forever.

CHAPTER XVII

After that midnight parting the first thing I can recall was the touch of a gentle hand upon my face. When my eyes opened I saw Hester bending over me.

"You are at home now, Kendric," said she. Such a feeling of weakness came over me that I could not speak. I thought a nail had been driven into my brain, but the tears that began rolling down my cheeks and the moans that broke from my lips seemed to loosen it.

Many days passed before I was able to reflect upon this last tragic episode in my life or to take any thought of the morrow. One evening I awoke from a deep sleep feeling a new interest in life. There were people sitting in the room and talking in low tones.

"Has he asked for Rayel yet?" said one of them.

"Not yet," was the answer.

"Better not let him know about it yet. There's time enough. He'll be around soon."

I called to them and they came quickly to my bedside. There were Hester and Mr. Earl and his good wife, all looking down upon me with smiling faces.

"You need not be afraid to tell me now. I know that Rayel is dead."

They made no answer.

"I know he is dead, but tell me how it happened," I said. "There is no danger; I am quite strong now."

Mr. Earl took my hand and told me in a low, calm voice, all he knew of the tragedy. He only knew, however, that the lamp had exploded and that Rayel had been horribly burned by the oil.

"I suppose," said he, "that the lamp was on a table near his bed when it exploded. In a moment the whole room was afire, and you, no doubt, being asleep at the time, he lifted you up and ran with you down the stairway and out of the open door. But in the meantime he had been horribly burned, and he fell in a faint as soon as he reached the pavement. Strangely enough you were unconscious for some moments, although you were not badly burned. Probably it was the smoke."

Then no one knows, thought I, what really did happen that night. The lamp must have fallen almost directly upon Rayel's head, and the oil had no doubt saturated his hair and clothing.

"And the house?" I asked. "Is that -"

"In ashes," he replied.

Then every trace of that strange event, which no eye save mine had witnessed, was wiped out forever. The hideous secret had better never be told.

"If I was not badly burned, tell me why I have been lying ill."

"Brain fever, my boy," said he. "Too much excitement, I presume - but you're out of danger now, and will be on your feet again in a few days."

Fortunately the latter assurance was rightly spoken. The first day that brought me strength enough to put on my clothes and walk about the house, Mr. Earl invited me into the library to talk business. We were no sooner seated than he unlocked a drawer and handed me a document to read.

It was a deed of all my father's real and personal property.

"They have both confessed," said he.

"Confessed what?" I asked, wondering if the secret of my father's death had come out.

"The conspiracy against your life. There were two accomplices - one Count de Montalle, formerly a servant of Cobb, and now a convict in America, and the other a man named Fenlon, who is under arrest. These were the men who tried to take your life. Fenlon came over on the steamer with you, I believe."

"And my stepmother - where is she?"

"Gone to answer for her sins at a higher court," said he. "Her last deposition is annexed to the deed. The old hussy ran into the fire like a miller, and stood there screaming, 'Look at that picture on the wall! Oh, God! do you see it?' she shouted to the fellow who found her standing in the smoke and flames. The chap was so excited he really thought that he did see the picture of a woman holding a knife."

"That is strange, isn't it?" said I. "Who was the man?"

"A detective," said he, "whom I hired to watch the house that night. He heard some disturbance, it seems, and, fearing mischief, he immediately forced the door open and ran pell-mell into your cousin, noble fellow, who was then bringing you down-stairs. If he had been one moment later the woman would have been burned to death, and we would never have got this deposition. Cobb wouldn't have been the first to weaken, you may be sure of that. But after she had told the whole story, why, there was no use in holding out. Badly burned? No, strange to say, she was not badly burned, but frightened out of her wits. The nervous shock was too much for her and soon led to fatal results. Cobb will go to prison."

I made no reply. I could not have found words to express the thoughts that came trooping through my brain.

"I have to tell you," he continued, "that your cousin left a will bequeathing to you his father's house and a number of valuable paintings."

I turned away and burning tears of sorrow came to my eyes. It was indeed a sad inheritance - the earthly part of his great riches - and of little moment to me. I could not bear to think or speak of it then, and I begged my friend to hide the will from my sight until time might give me strength to read it with composure.

One evening in early spring Hester and I were walking along the shore of the Mediterranean at Marseilles. I had been traveling through southern Europe since my recovery, accompanied by Mr. and Mrs. Earl. Hester had recently joined us in this ancient city of Provence. The sun was sinking below the distant horizon of water, and his shafts, glancing from the western edge of the sea, shot far into the immeasurable reaches above us. We stood in silence while the great wall of night loomed into the zenith, and then fell westward through the luminous slope of heaven. The broad terrace from which we viewed the scene was quite deserted.

"If it is a hopeless love I cherish, let me know it now, Hester," I said as we turned to go. "I cannot wait any longer."

"You can wait half an hour longer, I am sure," she said, hurrying me along. "We will be at home, then."

Some months after Hester had become my wife we received a call in London from our old friend, Mr. Murmurtot.

"You have been playing in a great life drama," said he to Hester, "and I, too, have had a part in it. Lest you may think that it was the fool's part, let me tell you that I am the man who arrested the Count de Montalle."

"And the man who brought Fenlon to justice?" I asked.

"The same. He confessed within three hours after you were introduced to him."

* * * * * *

Every week my wife and I visit Rayel's grave and strew

fresh flowers upon it. A tall shaft of marble marks the spot where he lies at rest. His name is graven in the stone, and underneath it are these words: "He was a man without selfishness or vanity."

Choose from Thousands of 1stWorldLibrary Classics By

Adolphus WilliamWard
Aesop
Agatha Christie
Alexander Aaronsohn
Alexander Kielland
Alexandre Dumas
Alfred Gatty
Alfred Ollivant
Alice Duer Miller
Alice Turner Curtis
Alice Dunbar
Ambrose Bierce
Amelia E. Barr
Andrew Lang
Andrew McFarland Davis
Anna Sewell
Annie Besant
Annie Hamilton Donnell
Annie Payson Call
Anton Chekhov
Arnold Bennett
Arthur Conan Doyle
Arthur Ransome
Atticus
B. M. Bower
Basil King
Bayard Taylor
Ben Macomber
Booth Tarkington
Bram Stoker
C. Collodi
C. E. Orr
C. M. Ingleby
Carolyn Wells
Catherine Parr Traill
Charles A. Eastman
Charles Dickens
Charles Dudley Warner
Charles Farrar Browne
Charles Ives
Charles Kingsley
Charles Lathrop Pack
Charles Whibley
Charles Willing Beale
Charlotte M. Braeme
Charlotte M.Yonge
Clair W. Hayes
Clarence Day Jr.
Clarence E. Mulford

Clemence Housman
Confucius
Cornelis DeWitt Wilcox
Cyril Burleigh
D. H. Lawrence
Daniel Defoe
David Garnett
Don Carlos Janes
Donald Keyhole
Dorothy Kilner
Dougan Clark
E. Nesbit
E.P.Roe
E. Phillips Oppenheim
Edgar Allan Poe
Edgar Rice Burroughs
Edith Wharton
Edward J. O'Biren
John Cournos
Edwin L. Arnold
Eleanor Atkins
Elizabeth Cleghorn
Gaskell
Elizabeth Von Arnim
Ellem Key
Emily Dickinson
Erasmus W. Jones
Ernie Howard Pie
Ethel Turner
Ethel Watts Mumford
Eugenie Foa
Eugene Wood
Evelyn Everett-Green
Everard Cotes
F. J. Cross
Federick Austin Ogg
Ferdinand Ossendowski
Francis Bacon
Francis Darwin
Frances Hodgson Burnett
Frank Gee Patchin
Frank Harris
Frank Jewett Mather
Frank L. Packard
Frederick Trevor Hill
Frederick Winslow Taylor
Friedrich Kerst
Friedrich Nietzsche
Fyodor Dostoyevsky

Gabrielle E. Jackson
Garrett P. Serviss
Gaston Leroux
George Ade
Geroge Bernard Shaw
George Ebers
George Eliot
George MacDonald
George Orwell
George Tucker
George W. Cable
George Wharton James
Gertrude Atherton
Grace E. King
Grant Allen
Guillermo A. Sherwell
Gulielma Zollinger
Gustav Flaubert
H. A. Cody
H. B. Irving
H. G. Wells
H. H. Munro
H. Irving Hancock
H. Rider Haggard
H. W. C. Davis
Hamilton Wright Mabie
Hans Christian Andersen
Harold Avery
Harold McGrath
Harriet Beecher Stowe
Harry Houidini
Helent Hunt Jackson
Helen Nicolay
Hendy David Thoreau
Henrik Ibsen
Henry Adams
Henry Ford
Henry Frost
Henry James
Henry Jones Ford
Henry Seton Merriman
Henry Wadsworth
Longfellow
Henry W Longfellow
Herbert A. Giles
Herbert N. Casson
Herman Hesse
Homer
Honore De Balzac

Horace Walpole
Horatio Alger, Jr.
Howard Pyle
Howard R. Garis
Hugh Lofting
Hugh Walpole
Humphry Ward
Ian Maclaren
Israel Abrahams
J.G.Austin
J. Henri Fabre
J. M. Barrie
J. Macdonald Oxley
J. S. Knowles
J. Storer Clouston
Jack London
Jacob Abbott
James Allen
James Lane Allen
James Andrews
James Baldwin
James DeMille
James Joyce
James Oliver Curwood
James Oppenheim
James Otis
Jane Austen
Jens Peter Jacobsen
Jerome K. Jerome
John Burroughs
John F. Kennedy
John Gay
John Glasworthy
John Habberton
John Joy Bell
John Milton
John Philip Sousa
Jonathan Swift
Joseph Carey
Joseph Conrad
Joseph Jacobs
Julian Hawthrone
Julies Vernes
Justin Huntly McCarthy
Kakuzo Okakura
Kenneth Grahame
Kate Langley Bosher
L. A. Abbot
L. T. Meade
L. Frank Baum
Laura Lee Hope

Laurence Housman
Leo Tolstoy
Leonid Andreyev
Lewis Carroll
Lilian Bell
Lloyd Osbourne
Louis Tracy
Louisa May Alcott
Lucy Fitch Perkins
Lucy Maud Montgomery
Lydia Miller Middleton
Lyndon Orr
M. H. Adams
Margaret E. Sangster
Margaret Vandercook
Maria Edgeworth
Maria Thompson Daviess
Mariano Azuela
Marion Polk Angellotti
Mark Overton
Mark Twain
Mary Austin
Mary Cole
Mary Rowlandson
Mary Wollstonecraft
Shelley
Max Beerbohm
Myra Kelly
Nathaniel Hawthrone
O. F. Walton
Oscar Wilde
Owen Johnson
P.G.Wodehouse
Paul and Mable Thorn
Paul G. Tomlinson
Paul Severing
Peter B. Kyne
Plato
R. Derby Holmes
R. L. Stevenson
Rabindranath Tagore
Rahul Alvares
Ralph Waldo Emmerson
Rene Descartes
Rex E. Beach
Richard Harding Davis
Richard Jefferies
Robert Barr
Robert Frost
Robert Gordon Anderson
Robert L. Drake

Robert Lansing
Robert Michael Ballantyne
Robert W. Chambers
Rosa Nouchette Carey
Ross Kay
Rudyard Kipling
Samuel B. Allison
Samuel Hopkins Adams
Sarah Bernhardt
Selma Lagerlof
Sherwood Anderson
Sigmund Freud
Standish O'Grady
Stanley Weyman
Stella Benson
Stephen Crane
Stewart Edward White
Stijn Streuvels
Swami Abhedananda
Swami Parmananda
T. S. Ackland
The Princess Der Ling
Thomas A. Janvier
Thomas A Kempis
Thomas Anderton
Thomas Bailey Aldrich
Thomas Bulfinch
Thomas De Quincey
Thomas H. Huxley
Thomas Hardy
Thomas More
Thornton W. Burgess
U. S. Grant
Valentine Williams
Victor Appleton
Virginia Woolf
Walter Scott
Washington Irving
Wilbur Lawton
Wilkie Collins
Willa Cather
Willard F. Baker
William Makepeace
Thackeray
William W. Walter
Winston Churchill
Yei Theodora Ozaki
Young E. Allison
Zane Grey

www.ingramcontent.com/pod-product-compliance
Lightning Source LLC
Chambersburg PA
CBHW031839170626
46807CB00004B/1532